HER FAKE-FIANCE COWBOY PROTECTOR

BROTHERS OF MILLER RANCH BOOK FOUR

NATALIE DEAN

DEDICATION

I'd like to dedicate this book to YOU! The readers of my books. Without your interest in reading these heartwarming stories of love, I wouldn't have made it this far. So thank you so much for taking the time to read any and hopefully all of my books.

And I can't leave out my wonderful mother, son, sister, and Auntie. I love you all, and thank you for helping me make this happen.

Most of all, I thank God for blessing me on this endeavor.

OTHER BOOKS BY NATALIE DEAN

CONTEMPORARY ROMANCE

Miller Family Saga

BROTHERS OF MILLER RANCH

Miller Family Saga Series 1

Her Second Chance Cowboy

Saving Her Cowboy

Her Rival Cowboy

Her Fake-Fiance Cowboy Protector

Taming Her Cowboy Billionaire

Brothers of Miller Ranch Complete Collection

MILLER BROTHERS OF TEXAS

Miller Family Saga Series 2

The New Cowboy at Miller Ranch Prologue

Humbling Her Cowboy

In Debt to the Cowboy

The Cowboy Falls for the Veterinarian

Almost Fired by the Cowboy

Faking a Date with Her Cowboy Boss

Miller Brothers of Texas Complete Collection

BRIDES OF MILLER RANCH, N.M.

Miller Family Saga Series 3

Cowgirl Fallin' for the Single Dad

Cowgirl Fallin' for the Ranch Hand

Cowgirl Fallin' for the Neighbor

Cowgirl Fallin' for the Miller Brother

Cowgirl Fallin' for Her Best Friend's Brother

Cowboy Fallin' in Love Again

Brides of Miller Ranch Complete Collection

Miller Family Wrap-up Story

(An update on all your favorite characters!)

∼

Copper Creek Romances

BAKER BROTHERS OF COPPER CREEK

Copper Creek Romances Series 1

Cowboys & Protective Ways

Cowboys & Crushes

Cowboys & Christmas Kisses

Cowboys & Broken Hearts

Cowboys & Second Chances

Cowboys & Wedding Woes

Cowboys' Mom Finds Love

Baker Brothers of Copper Creek Complete Collection

CALLAHANS OF COPPER CREEK

Copper Creek Romances Series 2

Making a Cowgirl

Marrying a Cowgirl

Christmas with a Cowgirl

Trusting a Cowgirl

Dating a Cowgirl

Catching a Cowgirl

Loving a Cowgirl

Marrying a Cowboy

Callahans of Copper Creek Complete Collection

KEAGANS OF COPPER CREEK

Copper Creek Romances Series 3

Some Cowboys are Off-Limits

Some Cowgirls Love Single Dads

Some Cowboys are Infuriating

Some Cowboys Don't Like City Girls

Some Cowboys Heal Broken Hearts

Some Cowboys are Just Friends (Coming July 2024)

Though I try to keep this list updated in each book, you may also visit my website nataliedeanauthor.com for the most up to date information on my book list.

CONTENTS

1

Bradley

"*A*nd here's to you, the best friends I could ever ask for. Your passion, and your even heads, help temper me to be a better man. The type of man who might just deserve Michelle."

There was a round of applause and Bradley lifted his glass, toasting along with his friends at his friend Christian's bachelor party. It really was a nice toast, but he couldn't help feeling a little... detached from the conversation.

It wasn't that he wasn't happy for Christian. The guy had been his friend since junior year of high school and was one of the good ones. He was also the last of Bradley's single companions, and that was leaving him feeling... strange.

Normally Bradley never really cared about being in a relationship, or romance, or anything like that. He had dated in college, but that had turned out to be such a debacle that it had turned him off from the whole idea entirely.

Besides, it wasn't like he didn't have plenty to do. Ever since halfway through his online college classes, he'd taken over a lot of the family accounting. As the months passed, more and more responsibilities were put on him until he was just as much a part of his family's financial and investment planning as the experts they kept on the payroll.

And he didn't mind his busy schedule. He *liked* being so vital to the Ranch. Sure, Ben may have been the lead for everything, but Bradley was the one who made sure the bills were paid enough for the eldest brother to keep right on doing his leader thing. He'd been content in that, knowing his value and building on it with each year. He didn't need a relationship.

But then his brothers started finding women, one by one until only he was left. Well, there was Bryant too, but the youngest brother of his brood was so busy catting around that he certainly didn't lack for any sort of company.

At first Bradley hadn't given much thought to Ben and Chastity's relationship. Maybe it would last, maybe it wouldn't, but he liked that his brother seemed more cheerful. Then a mysterious bombshell had turned up on the ranch one day and ended up getting together with Bart. *That...* Bradley had never seen coming. He found himself watching in a surprised daze as Ben proposed to Chastity. Then even Benji had started dating the youngest daughter of the only other ranch in a fifty-mile radius.

Should Bradley try to find someone? Was it shallow that he even cared that he was the last of the respectable Miller brothers to be single? He wasn't sure, but it probably wasn't the right time to think about it during his friend's bachelor party.

"You okay there, Brad?" one of Christian's cousins asked. Jacob, maybe? Bradley couldn't quite recall.

"Bradley," he corrected. "And I'm fine. Just a lot on my mind."

"Ah, you got a missus who's pressing you for a ring?"

Bradley shook his head. "Nah, nothing like that."

The man nodded and clapped his back. Bradley couldn't help but bristle. While he was never anti-social, he didn't really like strangers infringing on his space and acting overly familiar. It felt... fake?

Maybe it was left over from high school. Bradley had always been the quiet one of the Miller boys, and it wasn't until he'd gotten involved with the drama club that he'd sort of come out of his shell.

But his quietness had never stopped other people from trying to befriend one of the Miller sons. They would be cheery and so nice to him, then turn around and make fun of or bully his friends who were also in theater.

He'd ended up in quite a few fights that probably didn't have to involve fists, but invariably did. It wasn't that Bradley liked violence, it was just that he burned so hotly, from his head to his feet, and he *had* to defend his friends.

"I hear you're some sort of financial whiz, is that right?"

Bradley shrugged. "I get by."

"I'd say. Christian said you managed to organize his whole party for less than a couple hundred, and that you took care of it all. Sounds like you two are real pals."

"We were in theater together," Bradley answered, finishing off his glass of whisky neat and standing up.

Arranging the bachelor party accommodations had been easy. It had been a pretty easy task, he'd called in some favors, offered some of the overflow from Ma's garden, and cash on the spot. He'd rented out half of the local tavern along with several of the rooms upstairs for the fifteen of them to drink, play pool, darts, and sing along to terrible country karaoke. Not that Bradley didn't like country; he loved older classics such as Johnny Cash and Gordon Lightfoot. He just didn't always appreciate hearing how his friends sang those familiar melodies.

"He's good people," Bradley continued.

"That he is, best of my cousins. Although I gotta admit, I sure resented being compared to him when I was younger. I'm sure you know what that's like."

"I suppose. Thankfully, I found my niche. But I'm going to wish my best to the groom and hit the hay."

"What? But it's so early!" the man objected, looking border-line offended.

"I know, but we get up early on the ranch. I'm sure you understand."

"Uh, yeah, sure. I'll go get Christian for you once he's done with his song."

Bradley looked over to see that the groom had moved over to the karaoke station, where his two younger brothers were egging him on to sing a song that was *definitely* out of his range.

Ugh.

"You know, I think I'll just text him," Bradley said with a sigh, not willing to put himself through two verses, three choruses, a bridge, and a reprise.

"Hey buddy, are you okay?"

"Yeah, just tired."

"Alright. Well, it was good to meet you."

The man held out his hand, and Bradley gave it a shake before heading up the stairs towards his own room.

While he had covered the expense of the entire bachelor party for his friend, he hadn't been entirely selfless. He'd gotten himself one of the bigger rooms, a suite, set farther away from the rest of the crew.

It wasn't that he didn't like them, it was just that he really was tired and he only had so much he could tolerate with so many people in one place. Maybe one of the reasons he liked numbers was because they were quiet, they didn't overwhelm him and demand his attention all at once. Or maybe it was that being on the ranch, surrounded by only his family, had made socializing even more exhausting than it had been in high school.

"It was good to meet you too," Bradley answered belatedly, but the cousin was already gone, leaving Bradley to finish his ascent up the stairs and across the landing.

He'd made sure to check out all the rooms before the party started to be firmly certain that everything was fine, so he already knew the way to his special suite. He found his mind wandering again, landing on thoughts of whether he should date or not.

He'd thought he'd wait until he was in his thirties, but that was multiple years away. Admittedly, his whole disinterest in dating was probably because of Gloria, a girl he had dated in college.

Their relationship had been short but intense, and somewhere around the third date they'd gone out dancing in the city, and she kept ordering him drinks. At first, he thought it was cute, her trying to treat them even though his family was wealthy, like turning the normal dynamic on its head. But then he'd realized that she was definitely trying to get him drunk. He'd put an end to her shenanigans that night, but then the next week she tried again. He ended up dumping half his drinks and acting drunker than he was, wondering what her goal was. She kept trying to finagle him into compromising positions while she had her phone out.

He put it together that she was trying to get incriminating evidence to blackmail him, which was rather stupid. Bryant had been photographed with all sorts of people in all sorts of inappropriate situations, and they never paid off any of the people who tried to extort the family.

So, he'd ended it quickly with her and had decided that the whole thing was more trouble than it was worth. He still thought that way, but his brothers sure did look happy...

Bradley was so deep in his thoughts that he almost didn't hear the distinctive yelp of panic as he passed down the hall. But the second time it rang out, it caught his attention and he stopped in his tracks.

There, to his right. A cry for help! The voice was terrified and barely audible through the thick doors, but he knew someone who was scared when he heard it. This definitely wasn't an instance of noisy neighbors.

No, there was something serious going on.

"Someone! *Please!*"

There was no thought after that. The next thing Bradley knew, his body was pivoting on his heel, the other foot lashing out to land just under the handle of the door the sound was behind. The kick caused a loud thud, but the door didn't give, prompting him to give it another solid blow.

The door popped open, slamming against the wall and only then did Bradley come back to himself. He wasn't some action movie hero. He was the skinniest of the Miller boys and good at math.

But the scene before him had him forgetting all of that. There was a woman in the corner, curled so tightly that she was almost child-sized. She was crying, with her arms crossed over her head like she was avoiding blows.

There was a man standing over her, taller than Bradley, broad-shouldered and full of muscle. Bradley saw the raised belt in his hand and a burning, churning demand for justice rocked him from head to toe.

Somehow, he got his mouth to work despite the fact that he felt like he was on fire from the inside out.

"Hey, back off."

Ah yes, *back off*. Brilliant repartee. The large, muscled man was sure to be intimidated.

But the man didn't even pause, his arm coming down and the belt cracking through the air like lightning. Bradley surged forward so fast it felt like his brain was left behind at the door, grabbing the man's arm and shoving him as best he could.

The woman gasped as if she hadn't even noticed he was there, and the man turned on him too, eyes flashing.

"Stay out of this," he demanded, looking down his Roman nose at Bradley.

"No," Bradley said, wishing he had a clever retort, but there was nothing. His entire brain was dedicated to protecting the woman huddled against the wall, so enveloped in her oversized clothing that he couldn't really pick out a single detail of her appearance.

"No?" the man repeated as if he was shocked.

"*No*," Bradley answered, stepping forward right into his space. He didn't know what was dictating his actions. The biggest fight he'd been in during the past decade was with a particularly stubborn bull who had a bit of an attitude.

The man surged forward, ready to barrel through the smaller, more lithe Bradley, but the Miller son brought up his arms. They clashed together, without any blows, shoving each other but neither gaining traction.

It took longer than Bradley would like to admit for logic to get to him, the violent man shoving at his chest like he was trying to drive the Miller into the wall. Yanking his shirt free from the man's grasp, he stepped to the side and twisted, the attacker stumbling a few steps forward.

Bradley took the chance to plant his foot on the small of the man's back and give him a forceful shove. It did what he hoped, sending the larger male stumbling to the ground.

Somehow, some part of his mind reminded him that he didn't actually *like* violence, and his arm whipped out, grabbing the door and slamming it shut before the man could get to his feet. Throwing himself against it, he went to lock it, before remembering that he was the one who broke the handle when he'd kicked the door in.

"Hey, I don't know who you are," Bradley said through the door. "But I'm here with a whole crew, and I'm about to call the cops. If you want to get out of here, you should do it now."

The man threw himself against the door, rattling the whole thing, but Bradley held it firmly.

"He's not going to give up," the woman rasped from the corner, struggling to her feet.

She was shaking hard enough almost to the point of vibrating, and he was worried about her passing out. His instincts were screaming at him to go help her, to make sure that she was alright, but he couldn't hold the door and help her up at the same time.

It was a fierce tug of war inside of him for several minutes, torn between the two impulses, until finally, it was too much. When he heard the man step back for another charge, he threw the door open and stared him down.

"*Stop!*" Bradley ordered with as much strength in his voice as he could.

Something in his tone must have worked because the man skidded to a stop and gave him one more long, long look before spitting right at Bradley's feet.

"I'll be back later, Soft."

Soft? Bradley didn't get a chance to ask what 'Soft' meant, because the man turned on his heel and cleared out like something was after him. Which was exactly what was going to happen once Bradley got his phone out and called the cops.

A thunk sounded behind him, and he whipped around to see the woman had gotten to her feet but was leaning against the wall. Had she stumbled? He rushed to her side, only slowing when she flinched away from him.

"Hey, I'm here to help you. Are you okay?"

"I'm fine!" the woman snapped, trying to push past him. But she wavered for a moment, her olive-toned face going pale.

Bradley caught her as she swayed.

"I'm fine," she repeated, wiggling out of his hold and grabbing the overturned table edge. "I have to go. I have to go before he comes back."

"He's not coming back any time soon," Bradley soothed, his feelings practically storming inside of him, demanding that he help, that he protect. Taking off his flannel, he draped it over the small woman's shoulders. It wasn't that she was particularly nude, in her oversized gray T-shirt and pajama pants, but with the way she was shaking, he hoped the thick and sturdy shirt would give her some comfort.

She clutched it around herself, pulling it tight like a cape, and finally, she let him wrap an arm around her. Pulling out his phone, he dialed 911.

"911, what is your emergency?"

"Hi, yeah, I'm at the Folsam Tavern, and some guy was just attacking a woman in here. I intervened, but he got away."

"We are sending officers right away. Is the woman injured?"

Bradley looked out of the corner of his eye to her, taking in the bruising on her face and arms and her swelling features. "Yeah, but she's up and mobile."

"Alright, please stay with her. May I have your information, sir?"

Bradley answered all of her questions as they slowly moved towards the door. The woman seemed to be caught somewhere between clinging to his form and trying to push herself away so she could handle herself. He didn't mind, however, and kept his supportive grip loose enough so she could step away anytime she made the decision to.

In all his life, he never thought he'd end up in a situation like this. It was definitely something his brothers—especially Bart—were made for, with their jacked frames and athletic pastimes. But still, he was glad that he was there for the woman at his side. He'd hate to think of what would have happened if he hadn't stopped to help her.

He guessed all those brawls in high school were good for something after all.

2

Sophia

The world was spinning around Sophia, making the floor tilt in ways she was pretty sure it wasn't supposed to. But at the same time, she couldn't even be that upset about it, because the pitching and churning and the pain in her head meant she was *alive*.

That thought alone was almost impossible for her to grasp through the pounding in her head. She had been so certain that she was dead. That she was going to end up as another statistic despite everything she had done to prevent that from happening.

That thought sobered her elation considerably. After everything she had done... it really had all been for nothing, hadn't it? She should have known better; she was too stupid to—

"Hey, we're coming to the stairs now, do you want to walk or have me carry you?"

That was the low voice of the man who had come to save her. Like some sort of avenging angel, he had kicked open her door and chased off her demon who was trying to drag her back to hell. It was hard to see through her swelling eye and the kaleidoscope of spinning colors, but from what she could tell, he really did look like a celestial creature come to save her.

Except there was no such thing as angels. And if there was a God, he wouldn't waste his time on someone like her.

"I can walk," she snapped. Or at least tried to. She had the feeling her words came out as more of a lazy slur between her swollen lips, but the man didn't comment. Instead, his arm held steady at her back as they slowly descended the stairs.

Suspicion rose in her with every step. Although the strange man was strong and beautiful, that did not mean he was good. After all, no man ever did something without wanting payment or recompense, no matter how shiny and polished their outsides were.

What if he led her to his room? Or some dark corner? Had she just stumbled out of the frying pan and into the fire?

But she was relieved when they reached the landing and he leaned her against the banister, letting her cling to that while he waved down an employee.

She watched, hazy-eyed, as he told the worker what happened. After a moment, he returned, helping her up and leading her where the employee was taking them.

They ended up in what looked like an employee breakroom to the side of the bar, just outside of the regular foot traffic, but not so isolated that she felt like she was in danger from the man who was still helping to support her.

"I should go," she repeated again, trying to put her thoughts in order.

The more time that passed, the more her adrenaline faded from her system, leaving her feeling exhausted and all syrupy in her head. But also, there was an undercurrent of familiar pain. The kind of hurt she'd told herself she would never have to feel again,

And yet there she was, feeling exactly the way she had so many times before.

"The cops are almost here, okay? And they'll be bringing an ambulance, I'm sure. You just gotta sit tight."

Cops? Oh, right. He thought they would help. Or he was one of them. *Was* he one of them? Well, no, that didn't make sense. If he was one of them, he never would have chased *him* out of the room in the first place.

Unless he was trying to trick her?

Her head throbbed, and she groaned. The man's grip tightened on her before he settled her into a chair, letting her lean against the table. She appreciated the cool wood against the pounding heat of her face, watching him as he crossed to the counter and wetted down a hand towel, then grabbed a water bottle from the fridge.

He turned to her but froze in mid-step, then turned and grabbed a straw.

"Here you go," he murmured, kneeling in front of her and unscrewing the cap.

Her vision swam, and the next thing she knew, he was pressing a straw up to her mouth.

"Slow sips, okay?"

She closed her eyes against all the spinning and did as he asked, enjoying the cool, cool water as it washed over her mouth. She swallowed it down greedily, ignoring the distinct taste of blood, and didn't stop until she felt slightly more human.

"There you are," the man said, putting it to the side. "Do you wanna wash your face up a little? I think you'd feel better."

She nodded, reaching out to take the towel, but instead he gently pressed the cloth to her forehead. The dampness of it felt delicious against her skin, and she allowed herself to sit still. Sure, this man might want something, but it was clear he wasn't asking for anything at the moment, and for the moment, she could use all the comfort she could get.

"Hey, I know you might not feel like talking right now, but do you know who attacked you?"

All of those pleasant feelings waned as the whole situation settled in on her again. Once more, her reality had shifted, because she was too stupid, just too darn *weak* to get away.

"I'm not weak!" she hissed, objecting to her own thoughts. She wasn't. She *wasn't.*

She tried so hard. It wasn't her fault that he... that he...

"You don't have to answer if you don't want to," the man continued, looking at her with those deep, chocolate eyes that looked like they could promise everything nice in the world.

"He's a bad man," Sophia answered softly, feeling her whole body start to shake again. It was like speaking about *him* would suddenly summon him into being right beside her. And this time, he would really kill her.

"Yeah, I thought as much. Did you know him?"

Sophia nodded her head, which turned out to be a mistake because her head throbbed violently enough for her to gag with nausea.

"Whoa, let me get you a trash can," the stranger said,

hopping to his feet and going to the nearest bin. By the time he was back in front of her, the gagging feeling had passed and she was mostly okay. Well, okay except for the dizzy thing, the pain in her head and her arms, and the squeezing feeling she had in her chest.

So... maybe mostly not okay.

But she would *live.*

"You okay?" the man asked, raising another part of the cool cloth to her cheek. "You don't have to tell me anything. You can wait until the cops are here."

But suddenly there were words rushing out of her mouth, thick and stuttered, but words, nonetheless.

"His name is Travis. Travis Wilcox." She took a deep breath, but she still felt so empty. "He's my fiancé—"

"Your *fiancé!*"

"Uh, my ex-fiancé." She fell silent at that, feeling shame creep up her spine with its slick, oily fingers. "I... I ran away."

"You ran away?"

She nodded. "We met when I was seventeen. He was seven years older than me and so, so mature."

She closed her eyes at how stupid she had been. How naive. She'd really thought he was some knight in shining armor, come to whisk her away from her dull high school life and treat her like a princess.

She continued, "He... he wasn't always like this. But he got hurt on the job and things started to go bad. At first, he would just yell at me. But then, I just... I just..." Her voice broke, and she hated herself so much. "I couldn't stop making him *angry.* No matter how hard I tried, I would always mess something up!"

"Hey, hey now, it's okay." The man leaned forward, almost

crowding in her space, but he stopped when she pressed herself further back into the chair. He settled instead on pressing the cool cloth to her face again. "It's not your fault."

"It took me years to think that I could deserve anything better, and just when I mustered up the courage to break up, he proposed in front of everyone we knew."

More hot, volcanic shame bubbled up in her as she remembered that exact scene. She had thought they were going to some sort of work event that ended up being a big dinner at a fancy restaurant with his family and hers. She remembered being utterly shocked, but then he'd gotten down on one knee, and everyone was cheering and whooping, and everything kinda faded away as she went from a girlfriend to a fiancé.

He'd really changed after that, like *really* changed, and she was certain that their bad times were behind them. But then she'd lost her job as a waitress, and he'd gone back to work after his injuries. After a lot of talking, he decided that she should stay at home and keep things clean and in order, make sure his lunches were packed and dinner was always on the table.

Until she started messing that up too. She didn't *mean* to, but it was stupid little mistakes, something a *child* could get right, but she just... couldn't.

"And so you stayed?"

Sophia nodded, feeling like an utter moron. Who stayed with someone who tortured them? An idiot, that's who. If she was stronger, if she had applied herself in high school like her mom had tried to get her to do, maybe she wouldn't be in this whole mess.

"That's alright. The important part is you're here now. Are you from around here?"

His voice was so soft, like a blanket, promising good things, kind things. The sound was a honeyed balm on her soul, but that kind of thing was dangerous.

Trusting was dangerous. That was how she got tricked in the first place. Caught up in a web of carefully crafted words and syrupy-sweet promises.

"No. I've been running from him for a year. Wait... has it been longer? I... I left in July. The summers were always the worst. He hated the heat. We lived in St. Louis, and even with an air conditioner in the top and bottom window, it was still sweltering."

She took a deep breath. "But he always finds me. No matter what, he always finds me."

"That's not right. None of this is right."

She shrugged; a bit amused at his adamant disapproval. "It might not be right, but it's just how it is."

The water bottle in his hand suddenly gushed, and she realized it was because he was squeezing it too tightly.

The show of physical strength triggered a wave of panic in her, and her fingers bit into the sides of the chair. He let out a surprising string of curses and quickly stood, grabbing another cloth to wipe away the slight mess he had made. Once that was taken care of, he had another bottle in his hand, straw already bent.

She sipped at it, looking him over, trying to figure out if he was a threat or adorable as he bumbled around her, looking like he didn't know quite what to do with his lanky frame. He paced, his hands clasping at each other, but his anger didn't seem directed at her. It put her on edge, but still, she knew... it wasn't directed at her.

"I'm sorry," he said.

She'd heard those exact words so many times that it made her flinch. Which in turn made him wince, and they were just a mess of random body movements.

He continued, "I understand you probably don't need this right now. I'm sorry, but people like that make me—" he cut himself off and shook his head. "I'm making this about me. That's selfish. Sorry."

She had no idea what to do with what he was saying. Selfish? What she needed? These were not phrases that came out of other people in an argument.

...or did they?

She was confused now, her head spinning, but the flashing of cop lights shining through the window stopped her from asking him what he could possibly be apologizing for, and her stomach dropped.

"I have to go," she said again. This time she managed to get to her feet but stumbled, the strange man catching her.

"Easy there, easy. I think you have a concussion. Let's ease you back into the chair, okay?"

"You don't understand," she whimpered. Ugh. She hated whimpering. It always drove Travis up the wall. He said whimpering was for babies, and she wasn't a baby. "You don't..." The words escaped her. "He'll find me."

"I promise you, I chased him off good an' well. He won't be back anytime soon."

"The ambulance..." It was hard to wrap her mind around what she wanted to say. There was a huge pit of darkness below her feet that swirled and churned and made her feel like she was going to sink into the nothingness. "He'll follow the ambulance. He'll *follow* me.

"What if I went with you?"

She blinked at him blearily, trying to figure out if she had imagined that or not.

"You want to what?"

"Go with you. To the hospital. I already chased him away once, and if I see him again, I don't think I'll be so partial to using my words."

It felt like it took her so long to understand what he was saying. Sure, his mouth was moving just fine and sounds were coming out, but they didn't make sense. He wanted to come with her? Why? It was one thing to be a good Samaritan and help her at the scene of the crime, as it were, but it was another thing entirely to treat her like some sort of escort mission.

"What do you want for it?" she asked suspiciously. Because he had to want something... right?

But his eyes went wide, and he looked completely shocked by what she said. "Want? Uh, nothing. To keep you safe? I just want you to get to the hospital and not be afraid."

Everything in her gut told her no, that it was dangerous, and he wanted a price that would turn out to be much more than she could ever pay. But despite all of that fear and uncertainty, she found herself nodding.

"Okay. You can escort me to the hospital."

He visibly sagged with relief. "Thanks."

Thanks? What a strange man.

3

———————

Bradley

Bradley couldn't remember a time when he had been so angry. Fury pumped through his veins like poison, making his stomach churn, but he forced himself to remain calm. It wouldn't do for the woman to pick up on his rage and get uncomfortable.

No. It wouldn't do at all.

By the time he pulled up to the hospital behind the ambulance, his knuckles were white. It made his stomach boil and his head rush. Her situation seemed so entirely *wrong*. It affronted his entire sense of justice, his desire to protect and do what was right.

When he arrived at the hospital, he was separated from her as she was whisked off into another room. Suddenly there were police in front of him, asking more and more questions.

Bradley tamped down his irritation with them. He understood that if they were going to help, they needed as much information as possible. So he told them all that he saw, all that he could remember. It was a lengthy affair, and by the time the two officers seemed satisfied with his responses, it was time for them to question the woman.

Bradley got the feeling that he probably wasn't supposed to be in the room with her, considering he was basically a total stranger, but he followed along behind the police officers and slid into the room.

And his anger ramped right back up again.

It was one thing to see the woman's injuries in the soft lights of the hotel. And another thing entirely to see them in the stark, bright lights of the city hospital. She had dark bruising along her face and far too much swelling. The abuse she'd been subjected to was wrong, and vile, and made him want to go find that man and teach him a *real* lesson. He didn't care that he was the nerd of the family, the math whiz. He was still a man to be reckoned with. And he'd use his knack for math to figure out the best way to knock that guy's block off.

"Miss..." one of the officers started.

"Sophia," she answered shakily. "Sophia Hernandez."

Her voice quivered as she answered, and it made Bradley's pulse shoot up that much more. She looked so small in her bed; olive skin sallow from her trauma. Her dark wavy hair was mussed, and it was only in the bright fluorescent lightning that he noticed that while one of her eyes was a defined hazel, the other had a pupil so blown out that her eye was almost pure black.

But instead of being off-putting it was... something else

entirely. Like she was a mythological being that wasn't supposed to exist in the mortal world.

It was hard not to scoff at himself with that thought. Now he sounded like those fantasy books he liked to read so much as a kid.

"Right, Miss Hernandez, we were told that you were attacked at the hotel. How are you feeling?"

"I'm fine. They'll be releasing me soon. Nothing but a few hours of observation needed."

"Right. We were hoping you could tell us about the attack."

"Nope. I don't remember a thing."

All three of the men in the room paused, clearly surprised. Bradley felt his own brow furrowed, and he stepped forward slightly.

One of the police officers tried again. "Mrs. Hernan—"

"*Miss*," she corrected quickly. "Miss Hernandez. Never a Mrs."

"Right, well, *Miss* Hernandez, we need your report in order to find this guy."

"Well, I'm declining on making one."

"What?" Bradley asked, unable to stop himself from walking all the way forward to her bedside. "Look, Miss, maybe you just need some rest. I know you've been through a—"

"There's no point!" she yelled, sitting up for a moment before wincing and sinking back down into the pillows. "There's no point. Just go. If the hotel wants to pursue damages, that's on them. I just want to get out of here."

The two cops exchanged glances before nodding. If they'd have been city officers, maybe they would have pressed her, but Bradley recognized them from the town. While there were all sorts of stories about corruption and bad apples in other precincts, his town had a grand total of five officers and a sheriff, and they all seemed fairly on the up-and-up.

Sometimes there was an advantage to small numbers. Hard to get away with anything when everything was more transparent.

"Here's our card ma'am. We ask that you stick around for a bit in case we have any other questions."

"Uh-huh," she answered in the most noncommittal way that clearly said she wasn't planning on staying in town. "Thanks."

"Be safe now. And try to rest so you can heal."

With that the two men exited, giving Bradley a nod on their way out. Once they left, he found the woman studying him with her mismatched gaze.

"What?" she asked, tone pointed and layered with exhaustion.

"I'm not quite sure what you mean by that," he answered honestly, sliding into one of the chairs so he could study her further.

His brain was wired differently than all of his older brothers. They all had their quirks, the three of them were all clearly meant for farm life. They understood animals. They understood working with their hands. They understood how to take things apart and put them together and be of general service to anything that was possibly needed.

But not Bradley. He saw numbers, figures, and ideas. He liked solving puzzles like budgets and statistics and riddles. So, when confronted with someone who was so clearly illogical— someone who didn't make the choices that were the most beneficial—his brain eagerly tried to figure out how he could fix it.

And this woman, this *Sophia*, wasn't making any sense at all.

"You're staring at me like you want something. And you followed me here. Nobody goes through all of that for nothing."

There was a bitterness to her tone like it was a hard-taught lesson that she'd been through multiple times. Bradley noted that in the back of his mind, then said the question that was lingering on his tongue.

"Why don't you want to report him?"

"I already said, there's no point."

"What do you mean by that?"

"I *mean* exactly what I said. You think this is my first rodeo? You think I was *born* with eyes like this? I've filled out enough of those police reports and restraining orders to know they do nothing for me. In fact, I learned a while ago that they usually give him a way of finding me.

"So, no. No report. No giving them my address." She paused and groaned, running a hand over her long dark hair. "Not that I even have an address right now."

But that didn't make sense to Bradley. The law was there to help people. Why would we have laws if they didn't help? He felt like there was something he wasn't understanding, and it was entirely due to his own lack of understanding rather than any error on the woman's part.

"Miss Hernandez?"

Their conversation stilled as a nurse came in. If the nurse noticed their wide stares, she didn't say anything and continued smoothly. "I need to go over some aftercare things with you, and we have a counselor who'd like to talk to you. Then you'll be released."

"You can skip the whole social worker thing. Been there, done that."

"Actually, we can't. It's protocol."

"Uh-huh, I'm sure."

The nurse's gaze flicked to Bradley. "I'm sorry, sir, but I'll have to ask you to wait outside."

But Bradley understood exactly why. He was some random male in the room with a domestic abuse victim. They wouldn't be doing their job if they let him stay.

"I'll be in the lobby," he said, looking to Sophia. "I'd like to make sure you get out of here safely."

"Why?" There was that sharp tone again.

He lifted his eyebrows and nodded once in her direction. "I like to see things through, that's all."

"Uh-huh."

It was that same unbelieving intonation she used with the nurse, but he got it. He couldn't even blame her really. With his own nod to the two women, he exited.

Maybe with a little bit of space, he could get everything figured out.

NOT MUCH CLARITY came in the two hours it took before Sophia was wheeled out to the front of the hospital with several papers in her hand. She looked more irritated than in pain, but he didn't know if that was a relief or not.

He also didn't know what he was doing there. Part of him said it was to support Sophia—after all, she'd been through quite a lot—but another part told him that she had no desire for his help. Really, if he was being completely honest with himself, it was more about satisfying his curiosity than anything else. And that reasoning made him feel uncomfortable, like he was somehow in the wrong.

"You're still here?" Sophia asked suspiciously when he approached her wheelchair.

"I told you I would be."

"Yeah, but that was before that counselor gave me the third degree. They're real worried I'm going back to someone who does all this to me."

"You aren't, right?"

She gave him a look, then rolled her eyes. "*No.* I just need to get to the hotel and gather my stuff, then I'll be long gone. I'm never going back to... to all that."

The nurse started pushing her to the front doors, which slid open. The moment she was past the threshold, Sophia stood up, groaning as she stretched.

"Dang, how much is it gonna cost to get a taxi back to the city? I don't even have my wallet on me."

"I'll take you," Bradley said before he could even think it through.

The woman looked over her shoulder at him. Although one of her eyes was nearly swollen closed, it was still easy to see the suspicion in her gaze.

"Why?"

"Why what?"

"Why would you do that? You've been awfully helpful for someone whose night I ruined."

He tried to look neutral as he answered. "I have to get back to town either way. It makes sense for me to drop you off."

"I... I guess that makes sense." She took a deep breath and looked him over again.

Her gaze was keen, knowing, and Bradley got the distinct

feeling that she was looking for weapons on him. She was going to come up empty because while the other brothers were handy with rifles or hunting bows, Bradley's only real skill was with a staff.

And even that was because he had gone through a ninja phase from ages ten to fifteen where he was obsessed with mimicking all the action heroes from Japanese movies and internet video tutorials.

"Alright. Thanks. I don't have anything I can pay you with."

"That's fine," he answered, pulling out his keys. "I moved to the parking garage after you were admitted. Why don't you sit right inside in the ER waiting room and I'll pull up?"

She nodded, and Bradley headed off. It didn't take him long to find his car on the upper floor of the parking garage, but getting out was the nightmare he expected. He was almost worried that she would think that he'd ditched her by the time he made it to the front of the ER entrance, but thankfully, she was sitting right there.

He unlocked the door and started to slide out, intending on helping her in, but she was already coming outside and jerking open the passenger side door before his feet could even hit the ground.

Right. She probably wouldn't be comfortable with him touching her. Personal space. While Bradley was probably the least touchy of his whole family, he was still used to tons of hugs and jostled arms and ruffled hair. It wasn't unusual for one of his elder brothers to throw an arm around his shoulders, or even for them to have a friendly tussle during family gatherings. So he was going to have to keep that in mind.

He needed to keep his movements slow and fluid. No sudden jerks or exaggerated motions.

Easier said than done.

He was concentrating so much about not bothering Sophia that he ended up silent pretty much the entire hour ride back home. She didn't seem to mind, however, huddled in the corner and looking out the window like she'd rather be anywhere else.

Eventually, they pulled up to the hotel. She jumped out of the truck way too fast for someone in her condition, and Bradley found himself rushing out as well.

"Hey, I get the feeling that you're pretty independent, but you're also hurt. Maybe I can help you pack up your things and bring them down the stairs for... wherever it is you're going to."

"I..." She hesitated.

Bradley continued, trying to look as non-threatening as he could, "Look, there are a lot of people in there, so you'll be safe. You can even stand in the middle of the lobby and yell up to me if you like. I just want to help."

"But *why*?"

There was that question again. "Because it's the right thing to do."

"Nobody cares about what's the right thing to do. People only care for what's right for themselves."

"Well, everyone's always said I got my head put on different, so maybe I'm just not like that."

Her stance seemed to only grow more firm. "*Everyone* is like that."

Bradley was trying to be understanding, trying to be non-threatening, but he felt like they were going in circles. "Look, I just wanna help. Can I? Please?"

She chewed her lip, wincing when her teeth bit into one of the splits in the tender flesh, and she sighed. "I guess I ain't got much of a choice. Yeah, let's go clean up and pack. I am *not* looking forward to trying to get together all my stuff after he trashed it."

Bradley nodded and followed her inside. The bar area was closed and roped off, but there was still a defined path upstairs to the rooms. He went at her pace, making sure not to reach out to steady her when he really, *really*, wanted to, and a few minutes later, they were at her door.

For a moment he wasn't sure how they were going to get in, but then she fished a thin hotel key out from her cleavage. Bradley looked away quickly, trying to be respectful, but the image was burned into his mind.

He felt disrespectful and mentally ordered himself not to think about her chest. Another thing that was easier said than done. However, the image did manage to fly from his head when the door swung open and they were greeted by a completely clean and empty room.

"Oh no," Sophia gasped.

He saw her melt in front of him. Suddenly the strong, prickly, five-and-a-half-foot tall woman was slumped against the door and shaking.

"It's gone. All of it is gone. He must have come and taken all my stuff. He... he's got *everything.*"

Bradley's heart sunk right down out of his body and somewhere into the crust of the Earth. "No, I'm sure the hotel wouldn't let him do that. Here, let me go to the front desk—"

"Excuse me?"

Both of them turned to see the same employee who had helped them before.

"Oh, sorry, ma'am. We decided to pick up the room. I hope the cops weren't too much of an inconvenience for you."

"No, not at all," Sophia said.

The hotel employee spoke in a hushed tone, her eyes flicking to the various injuries that were all over Sophia's face. "It was getting late, and we weren't sure if you would be returning, or if someone would be collecting your things. Either way, we figured you wouldn't want to return to things the way they were, so we cleaned everything up."

"W-what about my things?"

After seeing how Sophia stubbornly dismissed police and refused help, it was particularly crushing to hear the warble in her voice.

"We had spare duffle bags and a couple of suitcases that have been left behind over the years, so we packed everything for you. Apologies if that was presumptuous, but our owner said, uh... that you might want to get out of here fast."

Bradley didn't think it was possible, but Sophia sagged even further with relief. He took a step forward to catch her, but she just propped herself against the wall.

"No, no apologies. Tell him thank you."

"Her, actually. And she wants you to know that you're welcome to stay here, that we've banned that man who came in, but understands that you probably won't. She's... she's been through some stuff, back when she was younger."

"Haven't we all?" Sophia said dryly before nodding. "Thanks. I'll take my things off your hands and clear out."

"Follow me. We kept them behind the employee counter, believing that you might come looking for them."

"I appreciate it."

"Of course. I know things are often different in the big ol' world out there, but here, we take care of our own."

"I'm not one of your own though," Sophia objected, slightly breathless as they trekked back down the stairs.

"If you're staying here, then you are."

They reached the counter, and the employee opened the side of it to reveal three bags and a single suitcase. So that was Sophia's whole life? Everything she owned? The thought was mind-boggling to Bradley. He wasn't exactly a materialistic person, and even he packed more when traveling for long periods.

"You're not gonna try to carry this all, are you?" the hotel staff person asked.

"I've got it," Bradley said.

Sophia startled as if she had forgotten that he was even there.

"That's what I'm here for," Bradley added.

"And *all* you're here for," Sophia said.

She was regarding him with that same uncertainty that made his chest hurt.

"Yup, that's what I said."

It was easy to load himself up, carrying the three small bags by their straps in one hand and the rolling suitcase's handle in the other.

"Ready?" he asked, looking towards the door.

Sophia nodded and together they walked out into the night. Although it had been fairly early in the evening when Bradley had first tried to turn in, now it was outright late. He'd guess one or two am, but he hadn't looked at his cellphone since this whole situation happened. Even in the hospital, he'd been too busy pacing, puzzling it out.

"So, you want to call a taxi? Or do you need a lift to the station?" he found himself asking once they were standing there awkwardly for a little too long.

"I... I'm not sure. I need to look up tickets, but my cell

phone's busted." She let out a growl of aggravation that quickly melted into a broken sob.

Bradley stood there, completely shocked as her demeanor crumbled with every hiccupping sound.

"I thought I had more time. I tried, I really *tried*. I really did."

It was awful listening to her collapse in on herself, clutching her arms like she was afraid she would shatter into a thousand pieces. Slowly, carefully, Bradley set her things down and held his hands up.

"Hey... is there anything I can do to help?"

She looked to him with red-rimmed eyes, swollen lips pulled back from her teeth in a snarl. "I'm not *helpless!*"

"I know," he answered quickly, softly. "I know. That's not why I offered."

"I... I don't know where to go."

More sobs. He itched more than anything to envelop her into a hug, to ward away all the bad. He wanted to protect her. But he couldn't. He knew better than to touch her without permission considering what she was going through.

"I thought this town was small enough that he wouldn't find me for a while. I just had a couple more commissions to do and then I was gonna move right along, try to get a few more steps ahead of him, you know?"

"Commissions?"

"Yeah..." She took a deep breath and wiped at her face almost angrily.

He wanted to catch her wrists and stop the harsh way she banished her tears, but he couldn't. He could only stand there and watch. He never thought he would be so frustrated at having to use his words, yet there he was.

She continued talking, which he thought was a good sign.

"I'm a digital artist. I work for myself. That's the only way I can make money and not have him follow me. But I have to use a lot of pseudonyms and different names, so I can't really build an audience."

Bradley stared. Sure, intellectually, he knew that there were vile men who stalked and hurt those they were supposed to love, but he'd never *really* thought about it. How someone could completely ruin the life of another, from everything from having a place to live without fear, to having a job, to...well... everything. He'd never been in a situation where someone had such unlimited, merciless control over him, and he couldn't really imagine it either. But staring at the woman in front of him, all golden skin and bruises that didn't belong, he knew that it was wrong. More wrong than anything else he'd ever encountered.

And she had nowhere to go. No one to protect her. She was up against this massive monster of a situation that didn't make sense at all, and she had to be so tired of running.

The words were tumbling and out of his mouth before he could even think about it. Heart thundering, he watched the woman's eyes widen the moment he spoke.

"You could stay with me."

4

───────

Sophia

"**W**hat?"

Sophia had been through a lot, and she still had some painkillers pumping through her system, but she knew there was no way this stranger had just offered her to live with him.

Did he think she was *stupid*? She already had one man who had taken over her entire life; she wasn't about to go running into the arms of some other one. She wasn't desperate.

She wasn't *weak*.

No matter what *he* said.

The man put his hands up. "Wait, not exactly with just me. I meant the ranch."

She narrowed her gaze at him as much as she could, trying to read him again. While she had been so, so gullible when she was younger, years of being with *him* made her very good at reading people. She knew when to tell if he was just grumpy or if he was in a mood that would hurt her. It turned out that hypervigilance to emotion was extremely helpful in the real world.

This stranger's hands were up, and his eyes were wide as if he was just as surprised by his utterance as she was. He had helped her an awful lot... maybe, just maybe, there was some strange reason he was doing everything, and he wasn't expecting anything out of her.

Yeah, and maybe pigs would fly.

But still, it wouldn't hurt to let him finish his explanation.

"A ranch?"

"Yeah, my parents own it. You're not from around here, but it's the Miller Ranch, kinda a local staple. You could stay in the main house with my folks if you want. Right now Missy is staying there too while Bart's away for a, uh, commitment."

"Missy?"

"My brother's girlfriend. I got four of 'em, but only three of them are at the ranch. They all have their own cabins now, at the edge of the property. So it's just Ma, Pa, Missy, Cici and me in the main house. But I can go crash with one of my brothers, or even some of my cousins that work for us."

That... that didn't sound *too* terrible. "Who's Cici?"

"One of my younger cousins who's taking a gap year and wanted to get away from the city for a bit. She's from Cali."

"And why would you do this for me?"

He scrunched his face and tilted his head. *He's cute when he's trying to figure out what to say*, Sophia thought, then chided herself for being distracted.

He stammered out some words, "I... I don't know. I just...

feel like this is the right thing to do. Ma helps people all the time, and she'd skin my hide if I let you go off into the night without a solid rest in a soft bed and a nice meal."

Huh. A ranch. That sounded like something that was rural. Out of the way. "How far is it from here? What's your land like?"

He seemed confused, but the expression quickly passed. "Uh, maybe a twenty, twenty-five-minute drive out of town. We've got a lot of acreage for our various projects. There's the main house, which is pretty big, then the lunch cabin, then the workers' cabins, then all my brothers' houses. It's a spread, that's for sure."

Sophia hated that she was considering it. But she was *so* tired, and the thought of a warm bed somewhere *he* had no idea about was awfully tempting. But she knew that taking help from anyone could backfire somehow later. They would either resent her freeloading or demand some sort of compensation. Traps were always laid with honey, right?

But what was she going to do? Her head was beginning to spin, and the painkillers were wearing off. Her face hurt. Her ribs hurt. And she felt *his* shadow looming over her, choking her with the thickness of his presence.

"Is it safe?"

Understanding dawned on the man's face and he nodded. "Ain't nobody getting on our property or touching anyone without permission. We're peaceful folk, but that doesn't mean we're pushovers."

Sophia chewed at her lip again, momentarily forgetting about her split lip but then being sharply reminded.

"I... guess that I could do that. But just for tonight."

"That's all I ask. In the morning, you can use one of our

computers to figure out your next move. I'm sure Ma will want to stuff you with a real breakfast too. She can be a little overboard about those things."

Sophia tried to envision it. When she was younger, she had an aunt who was like that. She'd lived with them for a while and always made sure the table was overflowing and everyone ate their fill. For a moment, she allowed herself to wonder how the woman was doing, if she was well, before shoving those thoughts out of her head.

They would only bring her pain anyway.

"That sounds... nice."

"I hope it is. Here, let me load your things into my truck. You just get in."

It was one thing to take an offered ride from someone, it was another entirely to agree to get into his truck and let him take her out to some remote farmland. What if he was carting her off to kill her? Certainly, she'd seen enough horror movies about dangerous things happening in small towns.

But despite all the doubt—the voices whispering that she shouldn't trust him, that he could be dangerous—she found herself having a feeling she could trust him. So she clambered into his oversized truck. At least the vehicle was shiny and expensive-looking. Serial killers didn't drive fancy, extended cab pickups, did they?

Besides, it wasn't like she had much of a choice. She couldn't sleep out on the streets, not in her condition. She'd had to rely on that skill several times since she'd fled, and it always required the ability to jump up at the slightest sound of disturbance. Judging by the heavy medication drop-off she felt rolling towards her, once she let herself pass out, she was going to sleep *hard*.

So, she was stuck. Put into another situation she would rather not be in all because of *him*. Even chased off and tucked into the shadows, *he* was still controlling her life.

Was she ever going to get away?

She was just so tired.

Slumping against the window, she watched the road as the stranger got in and started to drive. Had he told her his name? She couldn't remember. The night was starting to blend into that hazy sort of mush that happened after too much adrenaline and too little sleep. If only she'd finished those commission projects a couple of days ago, she would have been long gone.

Then again, ifs and buts were like butterflies. Pretty to think about but didn't do much else for her. She would just have to settle in and keep on her guard.

Besides, it was only one night.

That's what she told herself and continued to tell herself as they left the town further and further behind. The guy wasn't kidding; he really did live out in the middle of nowhere, and her worry about riding to her death only grew with each passing minute.

But before she had the chance to open the door and roll out while she could, the stranger turned onto a narrower road and passed under a faintly lit sign. It was old fashioned, maybe even a bit kitschy, but it was clean and definitely didn't look like it belonged on a horror set.

Miller Ranch.

Huh, so he'd been telling the truth about that. That boded well, at least.

They continued down the long drive until finally arriving at a large parking area. Almost like a lot at a store, except it was just dirt. The stranger went along the edge of that, however, then around the massive house before pulling up to a huge garage.

"W-wait," Sophia sputtered. "*This* is the main house?"

"Yeah. This garage used to be real crowded, but ever since all of my brothers built their own places, it's pretty much just for the parents and me. Oh, and now for all the presents they hide from their girls."

There was something strange about the way he said that. A bit baffled but tinged with bitterness. If Sophia had more energy, she might dedicate time to dissecting that, but she was so darned exhausted, the conversation would have to wait.

"Here, I'll grab your bags and take you up to one of the guest rooms. We have to be quiet, though, because it is a bit late. Much later than I'm usually out."

"*One* of the guest rooms?" Sophia repeated, sliding out of his truck.

The garage was twice as big as any apartment she had ever been in, complete with another massive truck, a golf cart, a riding lawn mower and an entire wall dedicated to storage tubs. Her mind tried to wrap around the fact that this was just the place for their vehicles, but it was sputtering out at the insanity of it all.

"Well, three of my brothers have all moved out, so Ma converted their rooms. Bart still has his addition to the house where he stays sometimes when Missy's off doing stuff—he doesn't do the greatest on his own—but it usually sits empty. So, Missy's probably there, Cici is in Ben's old room, I'm sure, so that leaves two that should be open."

Sophia shook her head, trying to envision the inside of the house from the quick glimpse she had of the outside. She knew there was a wrap-around porch in the front, and what looked like a large balcony area on the second floor, but still... there had to be at least eight rooms in the house *minimum,* and she'd never lived anywhere beyond a four bedroom.

"That's... that's just insane."

"Is it?" Bradley asked genuinely, turning to give her a curious look before pressing a button to close the garage door and opening a wood door that she assumed lead into the house.

Sure enough it did, to a small, welcoming room with multiple hooks on one wall all painted different colors, and what looked like a shoe rack on the floor. There were also several plastic floor guards against the other wall with a few pairs of thoroughly muddied boots on it.

"Shoes off, please. Ma's a bit particular."

Sophia nodded. She rarely wore shoes indoors. It didn't make sense to track all the nastiness and schmutz from outside over clean floors. But if there was a mud room, that meant there were at least nine rooms in the house, and considering that four teenaged boys had once lived in the place, there had to be at least *ten* rooms. That almost made her brain short out entirely.

"So, it's probably gonna be pretty dark inside, does your phone flashlight still work?"

Sophia shook her head. Even if it did, the thing was long since dead. It'd been in battery saver mode all the way back before *he* had barged into her room.

"Alright, reach into my side pocket and grab my phone. Code's 3128."

She stared at him with wide eyes. Just like that, he was giving her access to his phone? The guy was obviously loaded.

She could easily find his banking app or multiple other choices and take a good chunk of change off him.

But he didn't even seem to think of that. Either this guy was an idiot—and he certainly didn't *seem* like an idiot—or he trusted her.

That made no sense whatsoever.

"Ready?" he asked, his free hand on the door.

Sophia nodded again, not sure her words were going to work for her, and then they stepped right into his rustic mansion.

"Huh, I thought the lights would be out," he said.

A feminine voice answered him, layered in the kind of way that only came with age. "And *I* thought my most responsible son would answer his phone at least once when I hear that there's been an incident in town!"

Sophia turned to see a short, solidly built woman standing in the doorway of what looked to be a comfortably sized kitchen. It wasn't the truly massive, opulent affair that she had been expecting considering the wealth she'd already seen, but it wasn't anything to sneeze at either. There was an island in the middle, and lots of cabinets, and what looked like two ovens and *oh!* a really nice dishwasher too.

"Ah, sorry, Ma. A lot of things happened."

"What sort of things that made you ignore my dozen or so calls?"

The woman wasn't yelling, but she was speaking in that stern sort of way that only some mothers had. Sophia found herself smiling ever so slightly. Men who liked to hit people didn't do so well around women like the one in front of her.

Maybe she was safe.

"It's a long story. Uh, Ma, this is Sophia. She's gonna stay here the night, alright?" The way he said it was so full of meaning that he might as well have waved a flaming baton.

Sophia wasn't sure what the woman saw when she looked her over, her wizened eyes scanning her quickly. Would she disapprove of such a low-class woman in her very fine house? Tell him that her home wasn't for a stranger who could steal their things in the middle of the night? Sophia couldn't really blame her for the latter thought. It would be real easy to make off with a good amount of valuables while everyone was sleeping. She wouldn't, but it was definitely something that could happen if she was a bit more desperate and a little less noble.

But instead the woman's serious expression dropped, and she stepped forward with open arms. Sophia tensed automatically, but relaxed when the woman's hands rested softly on her shoulders. She wasn't sure she was ready for a hug yet, even from a little old lady.

"Bradley Franklin Miller, you did not bring me a guest without giving me a warning to heat her up something, did you? I know I raised you better."

"I, uh, sorry, Ma. I guess I wasn't thinking."

It was nice to see him grow a bit red and flustered. There wasn't a hint of anger in his tone even though he was being scolded right in front of her. That wasn't like *him* at all, who couldn't take any sort of critique from anyone he deemed inferior to him. It made this man she was with—Bradley his mother had called him—slightly less dangerous in her eyes.

Slightly.

"I see you've been patched up well, but I bet you haven't been fed all night. I don't know about you, but a..." Her eyes skipped over Sophia's swollen eyes and busted lips. "A long night certainly works up an appetite in me. Come with me, let me get you something to munch on before we put you to bed."

Her tone was sweet, guiding, but firm. The woman gave the impression that there wasn't any saying no, but somehow not in a threatening way.

"I could use some food."

"Well, alright then! Why don't you pull a stool up to the island and I'll whip you up something right quick. You can call me Ma, or Ma Miller if that's a bit too informal for you. Now Bradley," she said, looking at her son with a much more stern expression. "You take this young lady's things and set up a room for her. Benji's old one should be open. Make sure to set one of our first aid kits by her nightstand in case she needs it in the morning."

"Right, Ma. I'll get right on it."

He gave a sort of "what can you do" half smile to Sophia then headed up the stairs with her things. For the first time since her night had been torn in two, she felt the faintest bit of hope. Sure, it could still go badly, but it was hard to imagine that would happen with such a nice woman fussing over her. She couldn't remember the last time she'd been taken care of...

"Now, do you have any food allergies I should know about?" the woman continued, guiding Sophia to one of the tall stools at the island.

"Just peanuts."

"Oh, good to know! One of my little grandnephews has that too. Terrible thing, a world without peanut butter! But I make him cashew butter and jam sandwiches that he goes gaga for! He's a sweet little man. Going to be quite the heartbreaker when he gets older."

"Uh-huh..."

Sophia just mumbled along, nodding as the woman continued with her polite conversation. The nice thing was that this Miller matriarch didn't seem to expect her to talk, mostly just keeping up a polite stream of words so the silence wouldn't become too overbearing. It was almost... normal, in a way. Like the woman was Sophia's grandmother, making a quick meal after a trip away too long.

Within a few minutes, the woman was microwaving a very full plate. "I normally only use this contraption for warming butter, but I figure you need your rest and it'll take too long for me to reheat it in the oven. But don't worry, this'll be the only time I nuke a full meal for you."

"I don't mind," Sophia said faintly, sipping at the water Ma Miller had pushed to her. And she really didn't. For the past few months, most of her meals had been dollar snacks or ramen cooked in the coffee maker at her hotel room.

"Well, you might not, but I certainly do."

The microwave dinged, and Ma Miller let out a pleased sound, taking out a steaming plate. She examined it closely, seeming to look for any cold spots, then set it in front of Sophia.

Holy... wow. Sophia hadn't entirely been paying attention to what the woman had been doing, and she certainly didn't expect the spread that she had in front of her.

It was all soft foods—because, of course, the woman had noticed her split lip. Mashed potatoes, some grilled salmon, baked squash and what looked like rice pudding. It smelled absolutely heavenly, and Sophia couldn't remember the last time she ate a real meal even close to the same quality.

"Ah! I forgot utensils. Not gonna get far without those, are you?" The older woman let out a little laugh then proceeded to set a knife, fork, and spoon in front of Sophia, which she hastily snatched up.

If the woman thought there was anything strange or uncouth about the way Sophia voraciously tore into her plate, she didn't say anything. She just busied herself with setting a kettle on the stove and readying some tea.

Sophia got about halfway through the spread before finally remembering to slow down enough to breathe. No one was going to take her plate away, and no one was coming after her for the moment. Once she got that idea settled, she slowed down and began to enjoy the food. It made for a much more pleasant experience, and when she finished, she sat back with a happy sigh.

Wow, she felt a lot less dizzy from those pain killers with a stomach full of good food. Who would have thought?

"Here, I brewed some chamomile tea. It should help you sleep. I understand if maybe some good shut-eye might be a little hard to get given everything that you've gone through."

"How do you know what I've been through?" Sophia said stubbornly. As much as she appreciated everything the woman was doing for her, she didn't like being pitied. She may be stupid, and maybe she was a failure, but she didn't need *pity*. "Maybe I got into a bar fight?"

"Maybe you did. But anyone who shows up at my house with the wounds you do has a story, and stories usually mean restless nights and broken dreams."

"Fair enough."

"Believe me, I've learned at least a few things in my years here on earth. Now come, how about I show you the bathroom so you can get ready for a good night's sleep. I'll make sure Bradley puts some night clothes on your bed. They'll be oversized because all my sons are strapping young men, but they'll be soft, that's for sure. And warm. Nights can get a little cool out here."

Ma Miller led her up an impressive staircase and then to a bathroom about the same size as Sophia's childhood room. Those times had been much simpler. Not easy, because there was nothing easy about being poor in a big city in America, but simpler. Less terrifying. Without the giant looming shadow of her ex constantly lurking in the edges of her vision.

"Feel free to use up all the hot water if you have the energy to shower, but don't feel bad if all you want to do is wash your face. I'll see you in the morning, alright?"

"Uh yeah, sounds like a plan."

"Perfect. We'll talk then, and you can tell me as much or as little as you like. I'll make sure that you're not pelted by questions the moment you come down. My brood can sometimes be... overwhelming."

"Thanks. For everything."

The woman patted her shoulder again. "Of course. You're a guest now in the house of Miller. Anything you need, you just ask, and we'll make sure you get it."

Sophia didn't know what to say to that and just nodded, watching the woman as she walked down the hall. Ma Miller paused at an open door and pointed in. "This is where you'll be staying. You go about your routine, feel free to use all our toiletries, and I'll go find where Bradley disappeared off to."

"Okay, goodnight, Ma Miller."

"Goodnight, dear. I'm happy to have you."

And the strangest thing was, she really did seem to be.

Sophia went about freshening up, washing her face, and spending far too long staring in the mirror. Her face really was a wreck. One of her cheekbones was swollen so much that her eye was practically closed. At least it was her blown-out pupil, the one that prompted people to make very tired jokes about David Bowie. But her nose was bruised all the way down its short length, and her lips were both swollen and split in several places. There were bruises and scratches on her arms, and she didn't have the courage to lift her shirt and look at her sides.

How had it come to this? She was so sure she'd gotten far enough ahead of *him.* That she'd been careful. Maybe *he* was right. Maybe she was an idiot who didn't know how to take care of herself.

Still, she would rather be a free, dumb idiot than one in his clutches.

But was she ever going to be out of his clutches? It seemed no matter how hard she fought, no matter how thorough her schemes, he always managed to find her. And the longer it took *him* to find her, the angrier he was. Maybe... maybe she should just go back—

No.

No. She wasn't going to go down that road. Nothing was worth being back with that monster. Every day full of stress, fear and pain. And the constant rollercoaster of walking on eggshells and wondering what the day would bring.

Besides, it seemed that—for the moment at least—she had a sort of safe haven for the night. Despite all his resources, there was no way her ex was going to come here and raid these rich people's mansion. And Ma Miller seemed like a force of nature all on her own.

Still a bit incredulous, Sophia finished up in the bathroom and headed towards her temporary room. She was happy to find a loose men's shirt and a pair of flannel pants sitting on the bed. Pulling off her old, bloodstained clothes, she was more than happy to shimmy into the new stuff.

Ma Miller had been right. They were *soft,* albeit comically oversized. She wasn't complaining, however, because it made the outfit extra snuggly, and she happily slid under the bajillion thread-count sheets.

Of course, the mattress was like sleeping on a cloud. She let out a happy sigh and finally let herself slip under. She'd never been a very lucky person, but maybe, just maybe, things were about to change.

She rolled over, laughing slightly at that. Best not get ahead of herself. One good night's sleep was not a reason to get all starry-eyed for the future.

But still...

It was probably going to be a great night's sleep.

5

———

Sophia

When Sophia woke up, she wasn't surprised to feel a deep sort of soreness, the kind that went all the way through her bones right to her heart. But what she was surprised by was that she was *comfortable*. Nothing in her life was *comfortable*.

Sitting up, she groaned as her body protested the sudden movement. She took a moment to breathe deeply several times before her mind kicked into gear and yesterday's events flooded back to her.

Right.

Wow.

The previous night fell like a dizzying slideshow of things going from terrible right on down to impossible. But it seemed that impossible was actually quite possible, because she was indeed sitting on an impossibly nice mattress, dressed in soft clothing, with the delicious smell of a *real* breakfast wafting up to her.

Maybe she was in a really convincing and lengthy hallucination. It made more sense than some guy showing up, chasing off her ex, and whisking her away to his mansion where a kind older woman tended to her and put her to bed.

Sophia shook her head, automatically reaching for her phone before remembering that it was busted. Right. If anything went south, she was trapped in a house very far from town with no way to communicate with anyone. That was less than optimal.

Well, the best thing to do would be to see if they had a phone.

Scratch that, the best thing to do would be to take some of the pain meds she'd been given from the hospital pharmacy. But she needed water to do that.

Putting together a plan of action, she went to the small plastic bag the hospital nurse had given her and fished out the pill bottle. Pouring one of the little suckers out and biting it in two, she set one half on the nightstand and palmed the other one to take downstairs.

Despite Ma Miller's warning, she was still surprised by the sight that was waiting for her.

The foot of the stairs led right into what had to be the living room, and beside that was the dining room where a whole *cadre* of people were eating and laughing and being the quintessential Americana picture.

She spotted Bradley first, of course, although she hadn't realized what a looker he was the night before. Maybe it had just been too dark, or maybe she had been too distracted, but the boy was certainly picturesque. He had broad, defined bone structure, the kind that models would die for, and deep, chocolate eyes that crinkled at the corner when he laughed. And he definitely was laughing.

Sitting beside him was a bigger, taller version of himself who had just finished telling a joke. That had to be one of his older brothers. The guy was broader, with green eyes instead of Bradley's dark gaze, and lighter hair, but the relation was unmistakable. Beside him a curvy woman with long, *long* dark hair and beautiful skin sat, talking animatedly with an even *curvier* blond bombshell who also was wearing an oversized nightshirt.

There was another slightly different copy of Bradley, an older man that could only be their father and Ma Miller's husband, a young woman with bright red hair, and two other young men whose backs were to her.

Sophia took a step back, the large group intimidating her, only to feel a small hand press gently against the small of her spine.

"Whoops, careful there! Didn't mean to creep up right behind you."

Sophia recognized the voice of Ma Miller and relaxed. Somehow, in just one night, the older woman had become a point of safety for her. She had that sort of comforting, assuring presence. One that Sophia wasn't very familiar with.

"Hey, I'm up."

"I see that. I was just about to go visit and see if you were ready to eat yet."

Sophia looked to the table, where she spotted eggs, bacon, sausage, muffins, biscuits, hash browns, and even some fried chicken. Oh, and grits too. It was a spread if she ever saw one, and once more, she felt herself start to drool.

"Yes. I could definitely eat."

"Well come on, I set a spot for you at the head of the table so you wouldn't have anyone right up on you. I promise we don't bite." She laughed and the pitcher of orange juice in her hand sloshed.

The humor helped a bit, and Sophia went to the open seat. To their credit, none of the people at the table stopped and stared at her. They just went on doing what they were doing, with only Bradley looking to her with a nod.

Wow, he really was *pretty*.

She didn't mean that in any sort of disrespectful way, but while all the other men around him were rugged, or jacked, or deeply tanned, or maybe even some combination of the three, he was lithe and streamlined. His hands didn't have the same callouses theirs did, and while his shoulders were broad, his waist was narrower, like a dancer or a martial artist. He was a bit of an odd one out, but it didn't make him lesser. It just made him stand out.

Without a word, people began to hand her dishes of food, letting her take what she wanted from them and load herself up. There was also toast and some greens and a bowl of fresh fruit. It was basically what she would consider a feast, but these folks seemed to treat it just like any other breakfast.

She had just finished getting a bit of everything on her plate when she heard several sets of footsteps coming down the stairs. Stiffening, she jolted only to see two more women coming down.

And they couldn't be more opposite from each other, could they? One was short and round, with truly impressive hips and thighs, freckles across her pale skin. The other was taller and slender, almost waifish. She was Asian, with her brown hair piled in a messy ponytail atop her head and full lips opened in a wide yawn.

"Hey there, sleepyheads," the blond bombshell said. "Bout time you joined us."

"Who you callin' a sleepyhead?" the rounder one retorted. "We got in at four am. Basically just had a nap."

"Well, whose fault is that for coming back so late from their road trip?" the darker haired woman at the table said teasingly.

"*Excuse us* for stopping and smelling the roses. Now, y'all gonna skootch to make room for us or make us stand here in our jammies."

"Alright, alright," the tallest of the Bradley clones said, standing up. "Scoot over now everybody. There's enough for all of us. We once fit fifteen people round this table."

"Forgive me for likin' a little elbow room," the blond bombshell said ruefully, but still standing and moving her chair.

It was all so... nice.

Which was weird.

Nice, but weird. That could describe a whole lot of the situation.

And yet somehow, besides the niceness and the weirdness and all of it, nobody asked her who she was or why she was there, or why her face looked like it had a fight with the broad side of a barn. And Sophia appreciated that. The less they knew about her, the safer they were.

In fact, the only question came from Bradley himself.

"How are you feeling?" he asked when most people were busy talking to each other or stuffing their faces.

"Better," she said.

He nodded, seeming to take it at that, and she was more than a little relieved. For being some sort of stranger in the night, he didn't seem to be that bad.

Hopefully, she wouldn't be around enough to see that change.

It wasn't until the meal was winding down, and half of the people had left the table, that Ma finally addressed Sophia.

"So, what are your plans for the day? Bradley mentioned that you need to order some train tickets?"

"Yes, but I need to research a couple of things first. And finish some work. You have Wi-Fi, right?" It was hard to imagine that anybody didn't, but they were far enough away from things that maybe this mega-family was really old-fashioned.

"Oh, of course. I'll write the password down and put in in your room. I do have to clean up a bit first, so girls, if you don't mind?"

She shared a meaningful glance to the women at the table, and suddenly Sophia found herself swept up in the klatch of women, each of them saying something right after the other.

"Ma mentioned your clothes are all packed up. How about we give 'em a wash and you can borrow something of ours?"

"You look like you're somewhere between Keiko and my size. I'm sure we can find something for you to lounge in for a few hours."

"Hey, I happened to just buy a brand-new skincare regimen from Korea! We could do our hands and soak our feet to pamper ourselves while we wait. Oh, I think there's a hair mask too!"

"There's a hot tub if you wanna soak, but we gotta cut some wood for the boiler."

Sophia paused at that last one, looking to the shortest woman with the wide hips. "A hot tub?"

"Yeah, biggest one I ever seen. The Millers had it special made since they have a whole brood of giant sons. Can fit all five of the boys and the parents too."

"Five?" Sophia questioned. "I thought there were just four."

"There are four who live here. The fifth—he's the youngest. He's not around too much."

"He's a bit of a prodigal son," Keiko added as if that explained everything. "But I have faith he'll come back to his family. They love him very much."

"Let's not get into all that," the shorter one said. "I'm pretty sure we have shorts and a tank top you can borrow for the tub, if you want."

The thought of warm water and soothing jets on her battered body made Sophia's knees weak. "Yeah, I'd like that. I'd like that a lot."

"Alright, then let's all go get changed. I'll have Bradley take your laundry to Ma while we're busy getting the hot tub ready."

That didn't seem right. "I can wash my own clothes."

"Oh honey," the bombshell said, her red lips parting in an impish grin. "We have no doubt of that. But if you think for a second that Ma'll let a guest in her house do their own laundry... well, you've got another thing coming there."

Actually, that made a lot of sense. "Alright. She doesn't seem like the type I'd want to pick a fight with."

"No, she ain't," all of the women agreed.

From there it was a trek upstairs, and then clothes were being shoved into her arms for her to try on. It was an exhausting affair, and by the time she was in a sports bra, camisole and shorts, she was more than ready for that hot tub.

But first, there was apparently the whole cutting-wood thing.

Sophia had approximately zero idea of what to do when they approached what had to be the wood cutting area, but the others seemed right at home. She'd learned their names during the whole clothing thing, and it was Chastity who stepped up first, her long, dark hair now up in a loose bun.

Chastity was the eldest of the group, and wife of Ben, who was also the oldest Miller son. She was some sort of big deal career-wise, but Sophia hadn't been able to quite catch the details of that. She seemed pretty nice, if not a little serious, and had a broad smile.

Missy was the bombshell, all blond hair and red lips and a laugh that could make anyone grin. Sophia had expected her to be a bit snobbish, a bit like the popular girls that bullied her in school when she was young, but the young woman was anything but. She was mischievous and honestly told the most awful puns. She was apparently engaged to Bart, the second oldest who had been in the military. Sophia sensed that there was more of a story there but changing in and out of their clothes hadn't exactly been the best time to investigate that.

The slender Asian was Keiko. Apparently, she was a church friend of the family and a very, very close companion to Dani—who was the red haired, plus-sized one. Church folk automatically made Sophia nervous, if only because *his* family had used their connections in their congregation to pressure her to stay with her ex. Said that leaving him would be a sin. That maybe, if she let him be the head of the household that he needed to be and honored him, he wouldn't need to... *discipline* her.

In her head, she knew that not all Christians were like that. That how they had acted actually went against the very Bible they purported to believe, but the connection was already burned into her mind.

Still, she doubted she had much to worry about with Keiko. The woman seemed kind and measured, meaning every word she said and saying everything she meant. She was almost the exact opposite of Dani, who seemed to have a constant monologue going on behind her eyes while saying less than a quarter of what she thought.

Strangely enough, even with all of the personality and info she had about the group of women, they almost felt... safe. That was an odd concept, but maybe it was because there was safety in numbers.

Or maybe it was because, even in the short time she had been with them, she could tell that all of these women were strong. Physically, in the case of Chasity, Missy (the guns on her were *insane*) and Dani, but also... more than that. Even slender, waifish Keiko had a confidence to her. One that Sophia was maybe, kind of, jealous of.

And strangely enough, being surrounded by these strong women, these women who knew how to handle themselves and chop wood and live on a Ranch filled with strapping men, made Sophia want to be less alone than she always was.

"It was my ex," she said finally, staring firmly at the ground.

She heard the ax pause before it could hit the bit of wood Chastity had placed under it, and for a moment there was just silence.

"The guy who attacked me last night. I don't know how much Bradley told you, but it was my ex. He's, uh, he's not a nice man, and I left him a while ago. But he doesn't want to let me stay left, so he keeps finding me."

There was movement, and then a gentle hand was on one

of her shoulders. And then a hand on the other. Then two more hands were softly gripping her own. When Sophia could bear to look up, she saw that all four women were connected to her, a look of pained understanding on their faces.

But no judgment.

How was that possible?

"I... I wish I could say that I left him after the first time he hit me. But I didn't. He promised me he'd never do it again. And I foolishly believed him. Then eventually, I was too scared to leave. I—"

"Hey," Dani said softly, squeezing her shoulder ever so slightly. "It's not your fault. We know those situations aren't so easy to get out of."

Sophia nodded. "I managed to start working without him knowing. Doing art commissions and saving up. But he, uh, he found out. And that... that was a *real* bad fight."

She didn't know why all of these words were pouring out now, but it filled her with relief, like the sheer weight of them had been building up pressure in her and she had been about to explode.

"That was when I left him the first time. I filed a restraining order, got my own studio apartment, and found a job. I really thought I was going to leave him in the dust."

She swallowed, dark memories playing over again in her mind. The fear. The feeling like an animal, hunted and trapped by someone far stronger than her.

"I was stupid. He broke into my apartment less than a month later. That's when he gave me a concussion and blew out my pupil. And... some other stuff. I was in the hospital for weeks, and when I got out, I went to pressed charges." She shrugged. "But eventually, the whole case was dropped."

"What? How is that possible?"

"His father is the chief of police in one of the biggest precincts back where I lived. He's got connections all over. So, when I finally realized that the authorities were never going to help me, I packed everything I could and ran. I've been running ever since. He's managed to track down where I am a couple times over the past two years, but I've always managed to give him the slip. Back in the hotel..." She shuddered, replaying that scene in her head. She had been so sure that she was going to die. Just another statistic where someone would ask, 'Why didn't she just leave him?'

Why was she telling these women all these terrible things? Now they were gonna judge her too. Think she was as stupid and weak as *he* said she was.

"I really thought that everything was over."

There was a silence for a moment and Sophia dreaded it, wondering what the women around her were thinking, wondering why she had ever opened her mouth. But then a sharp cracking sound filled the air, and they all sort of jumped.

Looking past Missy, Sophia saw Bradley carrying a laundry basket, no doubt taking it to the multiple clotheslines spread across a grassy hill. Or at least, he *had* been carrying it. Currently, the majority of the basket was on the ground with two cracked, plastic handles in his hands. Like he'd been so angry that he shattered them with his own grip.

Her eyes went to his face. She saw a struggle there. What struggle, she didn't know, but it was clear he was fighting some impulse. His gaze flitted to hers for just a moment, before quickly returning back to neutral.

Without a word, he grabbed the base of the broken basket, turned on his heel, and marched right back around the house.

"He must be going to use the dryer," Dani said helpfully. "Ma likes to use the clothesline for energy saving purposes. You know, the environment and all that."

Sophia nodded, but inside, she felt embarrassment swamp her.

She should have kept her mouth shut.

"Hey, I have an idea," Chastity said, stepping gently into Sophia's field of view and interrupting her line of sight to where Bradley had just been.

"Uh-huh?"

"Why don't you stay here for a couple of days? Then plan out where you want to go. You don't have to worry about your ex coming here, and you'll never have to be alone unless you want to. You'll get three meals a day and a nice bed to sleep in. Not to mention Ma's pretty great to talk to if you're ever stuck in an internal debate—well, and in general—but you know what I mean."

"I can't," Sophia replied automatically. She'd already been caught in the town and sent to the hospital. If he knew what county she was in, it was only a matter of time before he found her.

"Are you sure?" Chastity asked, just as gentle as before. "Or are you saying that because you're scared? Because I under-stand being scared. And I understand feeling powerless. You won't be that here, though. You'll have all of us and even more that you haven't seen yet."

As if taking that as her cue, Dani stepped away from their circle and started chopping wood again. Sophia could see the cords of muscle moving in her forearms. Missy turned as well, loading up large log chunks for the shorter woman to split. That couldn't be easy either.

Right. She was surrounded by strong women and rich people. These weren't poor folks that her ex could terrorize or even bribe. He could slip one of them a cool hundred and they'd probably just laugh.

Maybe... maybe it would do her good to recover a little, push out as many commissions as she could, and build up her nest egg again so that she could run whenever she needed to. And she would be lying if the thought of no ramen, Nutty Buddies or granola bars for a few days didn't make her stomach jump for joy.

"I... I guess it would do me some good to heal up before I hit the road."

"Good!" Chastity smiled and gently squeezed the upper part of Sophia's arm. "I'll tell Ma that you'll be joining us for a bit. No doubt she'll be thrilled. It's been a while since she's had new blood to fuss over."

Chastity looked over her shoulder and gave a few comments about how much wood was needed before heading back inside. Sophia watched, still too sore and tense to be of much help, until finally they had everything they needed. She did manage to carry a single armful of wood around to the tub which was much farther back than she expected, in a glen of wisteria, before the girls ordered her to rest. Not too much later, the tub was indeed bubbling and jetting, and Sophia was sinking in.

Wow. That was every bit as nice as she expected. Maybe it wouldn't be so bad, staying with these kinda intense, rich folks.

Maybe, for once, she could have a real rest.

6

———————

Bradley

He watched Sophia—a lot.

Not in a creepy way, or at least he hoped not, but she managed to end up in his peripheral vision quite often. He had been jazzed when Chastity had informed him and Ma that she was going to be sticking around for a bit. He knew he had no right, but he felt strangely protective of the woman, and the thought of her running off into the night with no money and a battered face made his stomach twist.

His stomach still twisted a lot anyway, usually whenever he thought about that monster of an ex that had beat her and played mind games. Bradley tried to keep his emotions level, but it was hard. He wanted to find that man and teach him a lesson. Or a lot of lessons. Ranging from *real men don't hurt the people they love* all the way down to *it is the responsibility of the strong not to abuse the weak.*

But for every day that passed, every day that he got to watch Sophia's bruises shrink and her cuts mend, his stomach twisted a little less. She was slow to open up to any of them, of course, and still about as skittish as one could expect, but he saw her start to accept that they weren't all about to pry into her business or chastise her for doing something wrong. Everyone in the house knew either the details of her situation or the peripherals, and Bradley was right proud of how they all were treating her.

No one took offense when she flinched away from a hand that moved too quickly around her, or how she would jump and yelp if she was startled. They'd even all taken to knocking against a door or wall when they entered a room to announce their presence, or walking a bit heavier than usual.

The only one who gave her a wide berth was Bart. He'd come home on her third day of being there after a round of sleep studies down at the VA, and apparently, Sophia's nervousness and terror was a big trigger for his own PTSD. No one told Sophia, of course, because it wasn't her burden to bear. The solution was that Bart visited the main house less often.

The opposite could be said about Missy, though. She was especially great with Sophia, like she trained in exactly what to say and do to disarm the woman or make her laugh. She was the one he liked watching Sophia interact with the most, and he'd started taking his lunches later, and on the porch, so he could see whatever crazy thing Missy was teaching Sophia next.

So far, they'd gone through some very basic self-defense, to tying different knots into ropes, into proper hand care for callouses and how to catch or run from an angry chicken. Bradley understood some of the lessons, but that chicken one definitely eluded him. Maybe it wasn't for any reason other than to be silly. It certainly was nice to see Sophia laugh, open and loud.

Several times Bradley wanted to go down and join in, take a break from his books, budgeting, and investments. But it was clear that Sophia was still much more wary of the men in the house than the women. She wasn't outright scared, or even frosty, but he could tell that she would always tense up. And he didn't want her to be tense with his family; he just wanted her to be happy. So he just stayed away for the most part.

But that became harder to do as the days passed by. At the end of five days there, Sophia had worked out a daily schedule. She would draw with her electronic tablet, no doubt working on those commissions she talked about, from breakfast until lunch. Then Missy and one of the other girls would usually join her for a mini picnic out on the front lawn, followed by lounging and then Missy's lesson for the day.

After that, it was more drawing until dinner. Then she and Ma would sit on the porch and rock on the swinging-bench while talking and listening to music or just sipping tea while looking up at the stars.

The more days that passed, the more Bradley got the feeling that Ma was on board to take Sophia completely under her wing. Wouldn't be the first time a Miller had taken in a stranger as their own, and it definitely wasn't going to be the last. But every time Ma even alluded to it, Sophia would insist that she had to move along before her ex and his family could figure out where she went. She would always say that the last thing she wanted to do was cause the Miller family any trouble after they had been so kind to her.

But that was just the thing. They hadn't been *so* kind to her. In Bradley's opinion, they'd done the bare minimum. If he had his way, he'd hand her a thick wad of cash and a vehicle stuffed to the brim with anything she might need, along with a map of all sorts of off-the-grid areas or protected places. The only issue was that Sophia would never take it. After one full week of living on the ranch together, he'd come to understand that she wouldn't accept anything she deemed "charity" or people pitying her.

She certainly was stubborn. It was frustrating that she wouldn't let him *help*, but he had to respect her boundaries.

"Huh, did we start to keep our record books in the yard, or are you staring at the pretty young lady again?"

Bradley jolted to see Pa leaning against the doorframe of his office. It had once been the attic, stuffed full of sports equipment and mementos, but once he'd taken over a good chunk of their financing, Bradley had it fully furnished and converted into his own space. Often, he'd spend entire days up in his office, living off food in his mini-fridge and passing out on his couch when the numbers stopped making sense. Eventually, Ma would come up with a full plate for him and bully him down to a real bed in his actual room, but she understood that researching and figuring things out for his family was his passion.

"Huh? I'm not staring." Bradley swiveled his chair back around to his desk, trying to look like he was busy, but for the life of him, he couldn't remember what he had been doing.

"Son," Pa continued, walking in further to sit in one of the plush chairs in front of his desk. "I've seen you go at these books and spreadsheets and numbers for a week straight with hardly a blink. Could'a boarded up all the windows and you'da been none the wiser. But now, well, I see you staring outta them. Since we ain't got any miraculous weather out there, I reckon the only real change is that frightened dove you brought in."

"I don't think dove is an accurate description for Sophia," Bradley said, trying to shift the focus.

But Pa just stared him down with that intense gaze of his. It was no secret that Pa wasn't a man of many words. He had a thick accent, and a stroke he'd had in his forties made the entire act of speaking often more energy than it was worth. He and Ma were opposite in that way, so the fact that his father thought that this was something worth talking about was... disconcerting, to say the least.

"Fair 'nuff. More of a raven, maybe. Did you know they're the smartest birds out there? And if you wrong 'em, they remember your face and tell all the other ravens about you? They know that there's safety in numbers and will mob whole predators or threats outta their territory. Only problem, Miss Sophia there ain't got her own murder."

"What?" Bradley said, startled.

"A murder. It's a group of crows or ravens. Thought you'd know that, seeing as you musta read every single book in the school library when you were there."

"Not *every* single book."

"Hah! Nah, you never were much of one for autobiographies, I remember that. Look, I'm pleased as punch to see ya looking at the world like you're actually living in it, but I gotta —" Pa's eyes narrowed, and he stood, walking over to the window.

Bradley turned as well, and that familiar stomach twisting started up again.

"Son, you wanna tell me why there's three city police cars coming up our drive."

"I don't know," Bradley answered, ice shooting down his spine. "But I aim to find out."

He turned quickly on his heel and rushed out of the office, sure that Pa could find his own way down at a more leisurely pace. Taking the steps two at a time, he burst out on the front porch just as the police cars pulled up.

Of course, his gaze couldn't help but flick over to Sophia, who was pressed up against the porch wall with her tablet and a broken glass at her feet. She looked utterly terrified, frozen on the spot and wide-eyed.

"Goodness, did I hear a glass break out—"

He didn't have to turn to know that was Ma coming out of the door right behind him. She took one look at the situation and crossed over to Sophia, picking up her tablet and setting it to the side.

"Come on, dear, why don't I get you inside? Bradley will handle whatever these people want."

But Sophia shook her head, her recently healed lips pressing themselves into a thin line. "I told you they'd come. I told you. I *told* you."

"Yes, you did dear. But don't worry. We'll take care of this, and you won't be going anywhere."

Ma picked up the throw blanket she had knitted off the back of the swing and draped it over Sophia's shoulders. "Come on now, dear. How about I get you a fresh cup of lemonade inside? Or maybe some soothing tea? I did just get a new willow bark flavor in."

They only took maybe two steps before the officers were filing out of their cars and a voice called out to them.

"Hold it right there, ma'am. We have business with Miss Hernandez there."

It was an older man who spoke. Not quite Pa's age, but with salt and pepper in his hair. It was clear from his broad body and stance that he'd lived a fit life and only recently had age starting to chip at him. But something about his face was familiar. Bradley couldn't tell if it was the set of his nose or the slope of his chin, but something about the man's visage rang a bell in his memory, which only grew louder as the man walked closer.

Finally, when he was almost to the porch, it clicked. The man looked like an older and slightly smaller version of the monster Bradley had faced off with in the hotel. This was part of the "family" that Sophia would so often warn them of.

Which meant that this man, whether he was a brother, father, uncle or whatever, was complicit in everything that happened to Sophia.

Anger bubbled up in Bradley and he took a step down from the porch, squaring his shoulders. "The way I reckon it, you don't have any business on this private property."

The man seemed surprised by the verbal pushback and held up his hands. "Whoa, no need to be aggressive here. Nobody's in trouble. I actually came to help. You see, I rode here all the way from St. Louis because Miss Hernandez there has a warrant out for her arrest. Pesky little thing, but it can be a real hassle down the road."

"What? No, that's not true!" Sophia said, finally seeming to lurch to life.

"'Fraid it is! Apparently you, lil' missy, failed to show up to jury duty. Lucky for you, it's a real easy fix. We just have to go down to the precinct and clear up this matter."

"Do you have the warrant?" Ma asked from behind Bradley.

"Well, not on me, Ma'am, but—"

"Then you come back when you have a warrant," Bradley cut in, closing the distance between him and the interloper.

A dark expression crossed the man's face, and he sighed. "Well, goodness, I came here out of the goodness of my heart. I didn't expect y'all to make things difficult for me. I know that Sophia likes to tell all sorts of wild stories that make her the victim, but believe me, she ain't as helpless as she seems."

The man started to pace, the other police officers gathering behind him. "She got a bit of a drinking problem, that one, and my family has been helping her ever since we adopted her into our home. She goes out and blows any money you give her, and if she runs out before she's done, she gets into fights. Real knuckle-dusters. She may be a little thing, but I've seen her take down full-grown men."

"That's not true!" Sophia snapped. "I don't drink, and you know it!"

He looked to Bradley, his gaze clearly trying to emote "see what I mean," but Bradley wasn't buying what he was selling at all. Even if he hadn't walked in on that... that... *monster* hurting Sophia, he knew a predator when he saw one. And there was no doubt in his mind that this man was a predator through and through. Even if he never laid a hand on Sophia himself, he enabled her abuser to get away with things.

"See? She's feisty when her temper gets going. So please, I know y'all are just good folks trying to do what's best, but let me help her. Let me take her to St. Louis, clear up her warrant, then get her into the rehab she needs."

The anger inside of Bradley was burning so intensely, so hotly, that suddenly it snapped. But instead of exploding outward, he felt himself go ice cold.

"That's a real good story," he heard himself say, low and perfectly calm. "Did you think of it during your drive here, or is it something that you've had a lot of practice saying?"

"Son, I don't—"

"I'm not your son. No, in fact, I'm pretty sure I caught your son in the middle of him raising a hand to Miss Hernandez over there. I'm pretty sure I had to physically *fight* him to make him stop attacking her. I'm also pretty sure that I went with Miss Hernandez to the hospital, where she was kept for hours because her injuries were so concerning.

"So you can take your faux concern and drive all the way back to St. Louis before I call *my* town's police and have you all arrested for trespassing, understand?"

The man drew himself up to his full height and the rest of the officers tensed behind him, but Bradley didn't care. He stood his ground, arms crossed and gaze hard.

"Now *son,* Miss Hernandez there isn't healthy enough to take care of herself on her own. As one of her legal guardians, it's my job to make sure she gets the help she nee—"

Then the ice broke and that fire was back, ten times hotter than before. "It's your job to protect her! To make sure she comes to no harm. I saw firsthand just the kind of care your son gives her, and I'll be dead before I let any of your hands on her again!"

Suddenly the man's appeasing demeanor disappeared, and his face grew dark. He closed the final distance between them so they would have been chest to chest if Bradley wasn't one step above the ground.

"You do not want to test me, *boy*. I have connections running even deeper than all the money you've got here. If you want me to make your life hell, oh, I can make it hell."

"You—"

"Stop!"

The wrecked cry from Sophia halted whatever words had been on Bradley's tongue. He craned his neck to look at her only to see that she had pulled herself out of Ma's grip and was staring them down. There were tears in her eyes, and she was shaking slightly, but the look on her face was one of a warrior.

"I'll go with you."

"*What?*"

Bradley wasn't sure if that was him or Ma or both of them, but it was certainly a shocked sound.

"I told you. I won't make trouble for you all after you've been so kind. You've given me a place to stay, but now it's time that I go."

She started to walk forward, and it was as if the entire world cracked under Bradley. Dozens of thoughts ricocheted around his mind, clamoring that he couldn't let her. That he needed to protect her. That all of this had to stop.

His eyes darted this way and that as she made her way down the steps, as if the layout of the porch would have some kind of clue. But it wasn't until Pa opened the door, a grave look of concern on his face, that a crazy idea popped into his head.

A crazy, reckless, *stupid* idea.

Reaching out, he grabbed Sophia's wrist as she walked by. It was the first time that they had touched since that night when he had saved her, and it was like electricity shot through his body.

Sophia stared at him, her eyes so wide even her blown-out

pupil seemed smaller. She was frozen in place, staring at him as if he were bigfoot himself.

"She's not going anywhere."

"Need I remind you, *boy,* that I am a legal guard—"

"*Were* a legal guardian," Bradley interrupted, his mind churning up words faster than he even thought he could think.

"Pardon?"

He cleared his throat. "I said maybe you *were* a legal guardian, but you aren't anymore."

The man took a step back, looking like a potent mix of confused, annoyed, and amused. "Uh-huh, and just how did that happen?"

Sophia was staring at him, her eyes boring through him. He didn't let go of her wrist, however, keeping it gently in his grasp. If she wanted to pull away, she could easily, but she didn't.

He didn't know if that was a good thing or not.

"It happened right about when I proposed to this wonderful woman." Straightening his shoulders and picking up steam, he nodded. "We're engaged to be married, and my fiancé isn't going states away without one of my family with her."

7

———

Sophia

𝒲 hat.
What?

WHAT!

Engaged to be married?

Sophia stared at Bradley for several moments along with everyone else. It was like someone hit pause on life with all of them reeling at the sudden revelation.

But with the speed that eventually came to all long-term trauma survivors, Sophia realized what the man was doing.

He was buying her time.

She didn't understand why. She didn't even understand when he'd had time to concoct such a plan, but she felt gratitude flood through her. Sure, maybe she didn't trust the handsome man entirely, but she certainly put more faith in him than her ex's father.

"That's right," she said, stepping closer and pressing into Bradley's side.

It was a casual sort of touch, something an engaged couple should be comfortable with, but it made her feel a rush of heat all along her skin, accompanied by a wave of nausea. Was she ever going to be normal again?

She continued, "I met Bradley here a couple months ago, and we fell in love."

Her ex's father looked like he was about to have an apoplexy right then and there. "You're... engaged?"

"Yes," Bradley's arm wrapped around her waist gently, and she did her best not to flinch. She couldn't ruin the ruse just when it started.

"Oh, my good Lord on high!" Ma cried, rushing forward and hugging Sophia fiercely. If her ribs hadn't healed so much in the past month, it almost would have been painful. "I thought perhaps something was going on! Now why did you go and try to keep it a secret from your own mother?"

"We, uh, wanted our privacy. You probably figured out that Sophia likes her privacy," Bradley said so smoothly that she was actually impressed. For looking like he had just been about to deck her almost-father-in-law, he certainly was collected again.

"That so?"

"That's so."

The man looked from Sophia to Bradley and back, his face becoming increasingly red. The officers behind him looked like they didn't know *what* to do. Sophia felt immense satisfaction seeing them flustered for once.

Bradley had been the only person to ever witness her fiancé in the act of hurting her. Before, people were only there for the aftermath, for the faded bruises and the scabbed-over cuts. She'd found excuses at first, but then when her family started to get suspicious, her ex had manipulated her until she ended up alienating all of them. It was easy to see now how he had isolated her, but she certainly didn't have that kind of foresight when she was younger. But the good thing was she had a witness now, first-hand, and that took away a lot of the power her ex and his family had over her.

"Well, I don't think I believe y'all."

Bradley stared the man down. "That's too bad. Now, like I said earlier, get off my property. If you want to handle this legally, feel free to talk to our lawyers. We've got quite a few of them, being a generational ranch and nationwide brand and all. And if you want to call the local cops, you know, the ones that have jurisdiction here, I can tell you right now that not a single one of them is gonna take a man's fiancé across state lines to go be with her abusive ex."

"My son ain't abusive! He ain't done nothing that she didn't deserve."

Bradley was about to punch the man, but the distinct sound of a shotgun cocking broke the entire scene.

Sophia whipped around only to see that Dani had joined the drama, holding a shotgun like it was no big deal. She wasn't aiming it at anybody in particular, but she wasn't *not* aiming it.

"Boy, I sure am excited for hunting season," she said loudly, giving Ma Miller a bright smile.

"Oh me too! But I do wish more of you would use those bows. Shotguns can really do a number on a deer. Makes me feel bad sometimes."

"Ah, you don't have to worry," Dani said brightly. "Most of your sons use bows instead. If I recall right, it's just me, Pa, Benji, Missy, and a few of the cousins who have shotguns. Oh, hah, and both of *my* brothers, of course. Man, that'd be some arsenal if someone ever decided to make trouble, wouldn't it?"

"It certainly would. Thankfully people here around these parts are so lovely, it almost doesn't matter that this state has the castle doctrine."

The man's eyes narrowed, and he spat at the ground at their feet. "Don't think that this situation is over," he said, his voice full of poison before he turned on his heel with all of his lackeys trailing after him and left.

Sophia watched with wide eyes. Had that really worked? Had she won that particular round? She never won any of her face-offs with her ex or her family.

But sure enough, the cars pulled out and headed down the drive, kicking up plenty of dirt and dust in their wake. Sophia wanted to do so many things at once. She wanted to dance; she wanted to scream in joy and disbelief. She wanted to throw a touchdown and lasso the moon and just generally run around until she couldn't anymore.

Maybe... maybe she was meant to meet this Bradley fellow. He certainly had done a great job of turning her life upside down so far.

But that thought brought her up short. Her ex was so lovely at first too, spending money on her, helping pay her bills, taking care of her when she got the flu. He made her rely on him until he was a habit, and once she was fully dependent, that was when things started to change.

So, as nice as these folks were, they weren't going to stay that way. That just wasn't how it worked in the world.

"So, let's talk about this wedding, shall we? I never thought you were the quick engagement type, my little Bradley, but it's just like you to have a secret girlfriend that you don't share with us until you're sure of things."

Wait, Ma's happiness wasn't an act? Sophia watched with wide eyes as the woman came back to her side and gave her another soft hug. She had thought the older woman's joy had been too over-the-top not to be fake, but the police cars were gone and she still seemed so thrilled.

"You know, he did the same thing when he was younger. Dated a girl for months, ended things, and she tried to blackmail him but kept it all to himself."

Blackmail?

Sophia looked to Bradley, begging him for an answer or a lifeline or *something*, but he just stood there, looking as bewildered as her.

"I figured you all were busy. Wasn't nothing I couldn't handle on my own."

Ma finally let go of Sophia and stepped away ever so slightly. "For having four other brothers, you'd think he'd be a bit more dependent, but my two youngest are all about taking care of themselves, doing things their own way."

She chuckled and wiped at her eyes. "Goodness! I've got to write an email to my list! We'll start sorting out details later. Now, I know you like to do things on your own, but I insist on no wedding until at least the end of this year! We're still planning out Benji and Dani's for goodness sake!"

"Uh, yeah Ma, not until the end of the year at the earliest."

Ma Miller clapped and headed inside. There were several exchanges from the rest of those present which fell on Sophia's ears like white noise. More than a bit overwhelmed, she mouthed to Bradley that they needed to talk. He nodded, but that did little to calm her nerves.

Why did she get the feeling that they had jumped out of the frying pan and into the fire?

8

―――――

Bradley

*W*hy had he done that?

No really, *why* had he done that?

He didn't know. He had been aware that the idea his subconscious sputtered up was insane and reckless and probably terrible, but it had been the only way he could think of to make those men leave, and at least stay away long enough for Sophia to finish up everything she needed to do. He hadn't exactly thought about the long-term consequences of his sweeping statement, and now they were crashing down on him.

It took a while to get away from the house. Apparently having a whole bunch of men show up and demand their houseguest—like some sort of prisoner—was plenty cause for conversation. Everyone had an opinion or comment on it. And if they didn't have anything to say about that, they wanted to talk about Bradley's secret engagement.

Alright, he really hadn't thought things through. But it had worked, hadn't it? He'd never expected his own family to buy it, and he came close to coming clean about a dozen times, but the thought of how crushed Ma would be kept stopping him.

Ma never asked for a lot. She wanted everyone happy and healthy and loved. He knew that she'd been worried about his complete lack of interest in anything outside of the ranch's finances, so taking that relief away from her seemed cruel.

He'd really stepped in it, hadn't he? Well, he was a math whiz, not a master strategist.

Eventually, when he and Sophia managed to get away, they ended up in front of the main barn, most of the workers having gone home to the night. Those who were around were all the way in the back, working with power tools that would keep them from hearing anything said from all the way at the green grass in front of the barn.

But the moment it was apparent that they were in the clear, Sophia whipped around. "What in the world are we going to do now?"

"I, uh, I don't know."

She stood in front of him with crossed arms, her brows furrowed as she stared him down. It was a far cry from the shaking, panicked woman he had found that first night in the hotel.

Then again... maybe it wasn't. Even bleeding and bruised, there was always a layer of steel to her. Right down to her core.

"Maybe we could just, uh, pretend to be engaged for a while, however long you need, then eventually break up. No harm done."

"No harm done? I think your mother just about died and went to heaven when she heard we were a thing."

"Yeah. I didn't really count on that. I thought she'd know I was making it up. I guess she was pretty happy to find out I had something in my life aside from our accounting books."

"And you're saying we could break up and she wouldn't be devastated?"

"Well, we could always play it up right before we end things. Make it real dramatic until she's relieved about the breakup."

Sophia let out a disbelieving noise, but he kept going.

"But the point is, it'll work for the time being. You said you needed a little more time. This'll give you that. Nobody's gonna haul off a Miller's girl. And even if they tried, the whole town would talk about it."

"This whole thing is crazy. You know that, right?"

"Oh, I am very, very aware. But sometimes, crazy plans are the best plans, right?"

She scoffed, but her arms finally uncrossed and her body language relaxed. "I don't think anyone will ever refer to this as the best plan in any regard."

"Maybe, but if it works, it works."

She nodded, and the conversation halted. The two of them stood there, and the reality of the situation began to sink in.

They were engaged.

Fake engaged, but still engaged. They were going to have to pretend to be in love with each other enough to get married.

Oh, boy. That was a *whole* lot of pressure that he hadn't exactly anticipated. Looking at Sophia, it seemed like she was getting just as overwhelmed as he was, and he didn't like that at all. The whole plan was to protect her, not to stress her out.

"What?" she asked sharply, using that same tone she had the first night he met her.

Great, it seemed like he had put things all the way back to square one. She hadn't used that tone since her second day with the girls, and he felt guilty that he had put her on edge.

But then she started to pace, chewing on the knuckle of her thumb, and it was all too much. He wanted to take her hands and soothe them, to tell her that everything would be okay even if he wasn't sure it would be. He needed something. A distraction from the situation and all the weight of it.

But what could possibly pull her mind from the fact that exactly what she had feared had happened, and he had only bought her time instead of solving her problem entirely? He should have believed her when she warned him. But he'd been so sure that her ex wouldn't go to such lengths. That it wasn't *reasonable.* Well, it was very clear that reason went right out the window whenever it came to those abusive—

"I... I need to not think. I'm driving myself crazy." She stopped pacing and looked to Bradley, like she was waiting for some kind of answer.

Right. He could do that. He might not know how to solve her entire issue, but he had an idea of how to lose at least an hour or two.

"Hey, have you ever ridden a horse?"

"A horse? You mean... like... a horse, horse?"

"Well, I'm not aware of any other kind. A few of our girls prefer riding in the evening, if you're game."

"I've never ridden one before."

He stepped forward and offered his hand. To his great surprise, she hesitantly took it.

"Don't worry. I'll teach you."

9

*S*ophia stared up at the massive beast that Bradley had saddled up and brought over to her. The horse was beautiful, truly, and everything that Sophia had seen in the movies, but she was also so *big.*

"Here ya go. Hyacinth is perfect for beginner riders. She's got a great temper and likes taking direction. Plus, she's on the smaller side, so she won't hurt your thighs as much."

"My thighs?" Sophia repeated, choosing to skip over the fact that this was a *small* horse.

"Yeah, when you're in the saddle, you control a lot of your body's motion by squeezing your thighs against the saddle. We'll go easy so you won't get any saddle-burn, but it's important not to let yourself flop around like a sack of flour."

"I... I didn't know that."

"Yeah, not a lot of folks do unless they have direct experience with horses. Now, let me show you how to get on."

He grabbed a short set of wooden steps and placed it next to the horse. Patiently, he showed her how to put her foot up in the stirrup and then swing her other leg over the animal. When he was seated properly, he made a dramatic little motion.

"Taa-daa. Now it's your turn."

Sophia licked her lips. All of her survival instincts told her that she definitely should not get on the giant animal that could easily throw her and then trample her. People got paralyzed from bad horse falls. She had enough on her plate without any of that.

But at the same time, there was something enticing about the beautiful horse. Maybe she'd watched one too many horse movies when she was younger, but it seemed like it would be mighty nice to be able to ride free, wind in her hair and all that.

"Can you show me again?" she asked nervously.

"Yeah, 'course."

He didn't even look annoyed as he gracefully got back to the ground and explained the whole thing again, making sure to stop at each step and make sure she understood—even when he had one boot hooked up in the stirrup and was balancing carefully on his other.

"There. Think you wanna try it? Ain't no shame in saying no," he said, smiling at her from up on the horse.

Part of Sophia wanted to say no. *Really* wanted to say no. But she was tired of being scared and tired of always retreating from things. She wanted to take some of the power back.

"Yeah. I do."

Deep inside, she felt a fledgling flicker of trust rise in her. This Bradley guy was alright. Although she couldn't guarantee that he would stay alright, she would take the moment for what it was.

"Well, alright then!"

He got down off the horse again like it was the easiest thing in the world then offered her his hand. Once more she took it, surprising herself, and let him guide her up the mini-stairs and next to the horse.

"Alright, foot in the stirrup. Yeah, there you go. I knew you were listening."

She smiled ever so slightly at that. From anyone else, maybe it would have been patronizing. But coming from Bradley's mouth, it was just... *sweet.*

Carefully, slowly, she went through the steps. It was much easier to watch than actually do, but that was often how life was. She bit her lip as she concentrated, finding her center of balance then swinging her leg over the saddle while also pushing up with her foot in the stirrup.

And then, just a second later, she was sitting in the saddle.

"I did it!" she said somewhere between a shout and her normal volume. She didn't want to spook the horse, after all.

"Never doubted that you would," Bradley said with a smile, taking the steps away before returning and taking the reins. "Now, I want you to squeeze a bit with your thighs to keep yourself upright. Make sure your core is tight and your spine is straight, but not rigid. You don't wanna be tense because then you're gonna bounce and resist the motion instead of going with it."

"Surely it can't be that simple," Sophia said, giddy with excitement. She felt so high and regal atop the horse, like she needed a crown and maybe a train. No wonder there were so many movies about them. Horses were *cool.*

"It's not, but you're a beginner and Hyacinth is *very* forgiving, so that should suffice for now. You ready to move?"

She looked down at the man uncertainly, but he was smiling brilliantly up at her, like she had made his entire day by even trying.

When was the last time someone had looked at her like that? She couldn't remember. No, her mind was full of scowls and red faces and shouting and—

She shook her head. This was a good moment. She didn't need to bring the shadows of her past into it.

"You don't have to if you don't want to. Nothing wrong with standing here a moment."

"Oh, no, that wasn't at you. I was just getting too much into my own head." Sophia took a breath. "Yeah, I'm ready to move."

"That's my girl."

Something bloomed in her chest when he said that. Something fragile and tentative and oh, so alien that she shoved it out of her mind with a vehemence. She didn't have the time or energy for anything new or unknown. She was too busy grappling with her current reality without going under.

And her current reality was that she was *on a horse.*

"Alright, here we go," Bradley said, most likely for her own benefit, before slowly walking forward.

Sophia jolted a bit at the first clop but remembered what Bradley had said as they headed towards the barn door. Adjusting her posture, she let herself relax slightly while still gripping the saddle. Oh yeah, her thighs were going to feel the burn later.

But later was later, because in her current moment, suddenly Sophia understood every weird horse girl she had ever met. Even though Hyacinth was just idly clopping along, not even fast enough to be considered a walk really, she felt so powerful and connected to nature. Weird, and definitely not accurate, but that was how she *felt*. Like there were no fetters on her. Like she could duck down and cling to the horse's mane and take off across the fields of Montana.

"There ya go! You're a natural. Do you wanna go for a walk all around the pond or just stick to around the barn for now?"

"The pond!" Sophia said quickly, maybe a little too quickly. It was best not to show how much she wanted or liked something, because then that could be used against her.

But Bradley laughed. Didn't judge her for being so excited to be moving at a glacial pace on the horse.

"Alright then, the pond it is. Normally I'm not a huge fan of geese, but the same ones have been coming here for generations, and they've been spoiled right rotten. As long as we don't go near their eggs, they should leave us be."

"Uh, are geese normally not nice?" They weren't exactly a common occurrence in St. Louis, only populating the mini ponds around the malls during very specific times in the summer, but the plump things didn't *look* so terrible.

Bradley laughed again. "Are you kidding me? Those things are basically piss and vinegar coated in feathers with a good amount of Satan pushed into their souls. Are you telling me you've never had one of those birds hiss at you?"

Sophia's eyes went wide. "They *hiss?*"

"Yeah, they definitely do. But don't worry, like I said, the ones around here are nice. Well, as nice as a goose could possibly be. Swans are the same way, you know, only meaner and more aggressive. It's like they know they're pretty so they can have terrible personalities."

Sophia found herself laughing, feeling so thoroughly

shocked at the mental images that were coming to her. "I'm learning so much today."

"Well, you're a city girl, right? There's a whole lot to learn about us simple country folk and our lives."

"Of all the words I could use to describe you and your family, simple would not be among them."

"Yeah, we are a strange set. How many families do you know that have five sons and give them all names starting with 'B'?"

"That's not what I meant, but now that you mention it, yeah, that is pretty weird. There a story there or something? Or does your Ma just love that particular consonant?"

"It's a family thing. Started about five generations or so ago. Apparently, it got into my some-odd great gammie's head that all of her children should have names that started with J, maybe to honor Jesus or something, and it kinda stuck. At least I was lucky enough not to be a double M."

"Oh man, I didn't even think of that. Has it happened yet, or have your ancestors been merciful?"

"Nah, Gammie Miller was real into comic books during the war—she was a nurse, actually—said it helped her forget about everything going on outside her tent. So she decided to give her kids the good ol' repeat initial just like a lot of her favorite superheroes. My Pa's name is Maximillian Douglas, and his brothers are Mack and McLintock."

"You have an uncle named McLintock Miller?"

"Yup. He has his own ranch down in Texas. It was going to be an extension of the family business, but he disagreed with all the pampering we give our animals and wanted to go grand scale instead of keeping it small like we have. Pa and him butt heads a lot when he visits, but they love each other."

It was interesting to learn so much about the man who'd rescued her, that she had been largely avoiding. She felt a bit guilty for that, but whenever she saw him, such a complicated mix of feelings rose in her. She was grateful, of course, immensely so. Some nights she would wake up in a sweat thinking that she was back in that hotel room, her ex standing over the foot of her bed.

But she was also suspicious. Trust was a luxury someone like her couldn't afford. If she let her guard down, and he turned out to be just as bad as everyone else, people would say "well why didn't you notice the signs?" or "you should have seen this coming."

And she was also plain ol' terrified. Regular ol' scared half to death. Every shadow could be her ex, lurking to take her back. Or some sort of new terror that she hadn't even imagined yet. Seeing her ex's father show up with a cadre of his cop buddies only cemented that fear, making her more paranoid than she was before.

Because if something did happen to her, it would be her fault. Or at least that was what people told her. Sophia still had a hard time separating what was real, good advice, and what was manipulation. Some people thought she should stay with her ex or somehow deserved what happened to her.

Because while that was easy to believe—that she was stupid and had 'asked for it,' and it was some sort of moral failing on her part that she'd gotten herself into such a bad situation— deep, *deep* down, she knew that most of the blame laid with *him.*

He was the one who chose to act how he acted, to terrorize her instead of discuss, to cut her down every time she tried to stand on her own. To manipulate her and break her down 'till she didn't know what was right anymore.

But now, she had gotten away, and she was going to keep on growing without him there to make her wither.

"You alright up there?" Bradley asked.

Sophia looked down to see Bradley glancing at her curiously over his shoulder. With the sun setting to the side of him, he looked especially handsome. Like some sort of Prince Charming from a fairy tale. And even though *he* had been all smiles and handsome at first, she couldn't help but wonder if this Bradley fellow was different. She was older now, and a whole lot wiser. She felt like she would be able to spot a wolf in sheep's clothing much better than seventeen-year-old Sophia.

No.

She was not going down that road. She couldn't. There was no room for handsome men or romance in her life when she didn't even have a place to live. She couldn't mix up her gratitude with affection. Those were two completely separate things.

"Just thinking."

"I thought we were doing this so you wouldn't have to think for a minute."

"Fair enough," she said, feeling her smile grow. "I think I'm ready to go faster. A real walking pace."

"You think so?"

"Uh-huh."

"Alright then, I trust your judgment."

Hyacinth picked up her pace, but that wasn't what sent Sophia's blood rushing.

He trusted her judgment.

He trusted *her*.

The thought made her dizzy, and that, combined with the freeing feeling of the ever-so-slightly faster pace, had her red-faced by the time they fully circled the pond. The whole scene really was beautiful, the last of the sun's rays disappearing from the water, making it turn from a shimmering, royal blue into the deepest, darkest navy bordering on black.

The bugs that buzzed during the day, and the countless farm noises, all began to fade gently, until there was only the swish of the breeze and a cricket every now and then, punctuated by wuffles or patient breaths from Hyacinth.

It was peaceful. It felt safe, even though that safety had been violated a few hours earlier.

"You look like you might have had enough. Ready to go in? I'm sure Ma will have a plate for you and a lecture for me on skipping dinner."

Sophia realized that she didn't want to go in at all. She wanted to stay in the moment, in the small bubble of peace for as long as she could.

But... it really was getting dark, and her thighs were protesting angrily.

"I... I guess you're right."

"I've been known to be every once and a while. Alright, Hyacinth, let's get you back into your stall."

He led her the rest of the short distance to the barn then "parked" the horse in the same spot where Sophia had climbed on. From there, he went and got the steps again, putting them beside Hyacinth and holding his hand out once more.

"So be nice and careful as you come down, swing your leg over and sit sideways with both of your feet pointed towards me, then slide down onto the top step. Take as long as you need. I think you might be surprised by how shaky your thighs are gonna be."

"Nope, I'm definitely not gonna be surprised at all," Sophia groaned, trying to lift her leg only for it to feel like a bag of bricks. Ow, ow, *ow*.

"Yeah, gotta get the blood back into them. The more you practice, the more your body gets used to it."

"Uh-huh, I'm sure."

Try as she might, she couldn't *quite* get her leg up on its own, so she grabbed the bottom of her jeans and yanked it up so that her foot caught against the horn of the saddle. Or at least, that's what she thought Bradley had called it. If he thought anything about her unorthodox method, he didn't say anything, just continued holding his hand out calmly in case she needed it.

With a little more wiggling, she managed to get her leg where she needed it to be and turned to face Bradley. She was pretty sure this was the kiddy way of dismounting a horse, but she didn't particularly care. All she had to do was slide from where she was in the saddle onto the top step.

It hadn't seemed like that big of a deal before, but suddenly looking down at the slight distance between her feet and the steps waiting below seemed ominous.

"Don't worry, you've got this."

"You seem very confident for the one who's not in the saddle."

"Come on, I'm right here if you need me. You think I'm gonna let you fall in my own barn?"

"...No."

And she didn't, she really didn't. Although she wasn't exactly what anyone would call trusting, she knew that—at least at the moment—he wouldn't let her faceplant on the ground.

Taking a deep breath, she pushed herself off and slid down. There was the tiniest of moments where she wasn't grounded at all and panic rose through her, but then her feet hit the top step and Bradley's hands came to support her waist, steadying her.

"Thanks," she said, letting out a breath she'd been holding. But after the shock of landing, she realized she was just standing there, Bradley's big hands holding her, strong, secure.

Terrifying.

She flinched instinctively, and it was like the moment was broken. Bradley stepped away, both hands up.

"Sorry, sorry. I should have asked permission."

She stared at him, surprised by his reaction. Didn't he want to tell her that she was overreacting? That she was being silly? That she should trust him?

"Are you alright?" he asked instead.

"Yeah, I'm okay," she answered quickly, although her brain was whirling like she had suddenly chugged far too much caffeine. "Just got a little startled, is all."

"Sorry about that."

"You don't have to apologize."

She finished walking down the rest of the steps and wiped her sweating palms on her jeans. Looking back up at Hyacinth, she had a hard time imagining that she'd really been on top of the beautiful mare for about an hour.

"If you don't mind waiting a couple of minutes, I can walk you back to the house. I guess I didn't take into account the sun setting and all that."

"Yeah, I don't mind waiting."

"Good." He smiled and the awkwardness from before faded. "Any good cowboy worth his salt knows to take care of his animal after they've taken care of you."

Sophia nodded, watching as he led the sweet horse back to her stall and went about taking off all the equipment he'd put on her. She had to admit that she hadn't fully been paying attention when he'd gotten the mount ready; she'd been too busy staring at everything in the massive barn and all the tall, mighty horses in every stall. There were giant black ones, spotted ones, even gold and almost-red. She had no idea horses came in so many colors. She really was learning a lot on the Miller Ranch.

Like, for example, once the equipment was put away, that wasn't the end of the job. Apparently, there was a bit of brushing, and some soothing words, and then refilling of water, more hay, and a treat.

It was comforting watching Bradley take care of Hyacinth. Despite the corded muscles evident in his arms and shoulders, he was incredibly gentle with her, voice rumbling and sweet as he told her how good she was and how much he appreciated her being nice to new riders. It made the center of Sophia's chest ache with... she actually didn't know what. Maybe one day, when she'd finally been away from her ex long enough, she could unjumble herself on the inside and remember what normal emotions felt like. Things beyond fear, suspicion, and distrust.

"There we are!" he said when he was all done, giving the horse an affectionate kiss on the length of her nose. "We'll see you again soon, alright my pretty girl?"

Hyacinth wuffled then turned to her food, clearly ready to relax for the rest of the night. Sophia couldn't help but chuckle at the expressive animal. She clearly had a personality.

"To home?"

An interesting choice of words, and she almost argued with him. But instead, she offered a nod and whispered, "To home."

Pulling his phone out of his pocket, he switched on the flashlight. He made sure to hold the door open for her, then shut it soundly before leading the way.

They were quiet the short walk to the house, but it was a comfortable sort of silence. One where she could be in the moment and experience what was around her. Or even replay everything that had happened on her first equestrian jaunt. They reached the porch *far* too soon in her opinion, and as she knew he would, Bradley opened the door for her.

"You have a good night, alright?"

She nodded, about to go in, before hesitating. "You know, sometimes I have trouble sleeping and I go soak in the tub to relax for a bit, and I notice there's still one too many rooms that are empty. Aren't you sleeping in your own room?"

Bradley looked sheepish as he answered. "Uh, my room is right next to Benji's, and we weren't sure you were comfortable with that, so I've been staying in Bart's addition ever since he came back. Him n' Missy are back in her cabin until she takes her next animal rescue trip."

Sophia's mind started whirling again. Lately, it seemed like it never stopped. "But why?"

"Why what?"

"Why would you go through all this trouble for me? I'm the one putting you out, costing your family food and time and bringing drama here."

There was that cute confused look again on his face.

"I don't know. It seems like the right thing to do. I want you to be safe, Sophia. And happy. And I know I can't just magically make that happen considering everything you have going on in your life, but if I can help, I want to."

"I don't really understand why you would do all this for me."

But he just smiled crookedly at her, and she felt that strange feeling in her chest again.

"That's alright. You don't have to. I just hope you know that me and all my family only want to do right by you. Really. We've actually got kind of a history of it."

"Oh yeah?"

He nodded. "Yeah, sometimes I'll have Ma tell you a story about our a-million-times-great grandmother who was hard of hearing, and the start of our adopted cousins which began with a lost heir as it turns out."

"You're kidding."

"No, I most definitely am not. You can ask Ma if you don't believe me, but make sure you have a couple of hours free because she *really* loves to tell those stories."

"Alright," Sophia answered with a laugh, finally stepping into the house. "I guess I better go about washing up and getting to bed."

"And being fed by Ma, don't forget."

"How could I?"

They shared a laugh, and that feeling within her only grew stronger, warming her from her nose to her toes.

"Anyway, I'm gonna head to bed now myself. It's been a long day."

"You know, we didn't really talk about what we were going to do about the engagement at all."

"No, but this seemed more important." He shot her a smile that, wow, that did something. "We can talk logistics tomorrow if you want. Good night, Sophia."

"Good night, Bradley."

He gave her another little nod then headed to a door that was next to the one she had first entered the house through a week earlier. Funny how that almost seemed like another life. So much had changed in such a short time.

But as he disappeared from sight and Sophia headed up the steps, the warm feeling in her faded and the shadows crept in. Shadows brought on by her ex and all the thoughts he brought with him.

Her blood began to rush, and that familiar sinking feeling began to fill her, until suddenly the lights flicked on when she was at the top of the stairs. She almost screamed, sure he had somehow made it into the Miller's mansion, only to see it was Ma in one of her flowing nightgowns.

"There you are, dear. Are you alright?"

Sophia let out a weak chuckle that sounded fake even to her. "Yeah, I'm fine. You just startled me."

"Sorry about that. But you weren't around for dinner. You hungry?"

"Nah, I'm alright."

"I didn't ask if you were alright, just if you were hungry. Ain't nothing wrong with being a slender woman, but it looks to me like you're not where your body wants to be."

She wasn't wrong. While Sophia had always been on the thinner side, she'd lost far too much weight from the stress and effort it took to stay away from her ex. She'd gained maybe a pound or two at most in the week she'd been on the Miller Ranch, and still probably had anywhere from five to ten to go before she was back to where she felt strong and healthy.

Granted, she couldn't even remember the last time she had felt both of those things. When she was nineteen, maybe? It was hard to say.

"Okay, I guess I wouldn't mind something."

"I thought as much."

Ma Miller trundled forward and wrapped her arm through Sophia's, walking with her down the stairs. And in the woman's presence, those dark, dark shadows shrank back to the edges of everything.

But even as Sophia sat on the stool and let Ma lovingly bluster over her, she knew that all good things must come to an end.

Eventually, the bubble had to pop.

10

Bradley

*D*espite the fact that he was fake engaged to a woman he hardly knew, things began to settle into a comfortable rhythm once all the excitement of the dramatic visit wore off. His family eventually got that the 'couple' was fairly private, and the more days that passed, the less likely it seemed that her ex or his family were going to pop up.

Sophia was hanging out and bonding with the girls even more, slowly growing calmer until she was able to get along with almost everyone. It was still very clear that she avoided most of the men in the house, but her shoulders didn't go all the way up to her ears any time a male walked into the room.

It was the small things he appreciated. Although a not-quite-so-small thing was that almost every day, Sophia would sidle up alongside him and ask if they could go for a ride. It made him feel important, in the same way that finishing a budget sheet or finding a lucrative new investment did, so he never told her no.

Not that he would have told her no even if he hated walking her and Hyacinth around. Sophia had become more important to him than she would ever know. And she had so much basic human decency denied to her, that she could have asked him for pretty much anything, and he would have found a way to get it for her.

Not that he ever told her how he felt, because that would just make her feel awkward and suspicious. But he was well aware of how much he wanted to... to...

Spoil her.

Yeah, that was the word for it. He wanted to buy her everything she wanted and shower her with everything she didn't know she wanted until she was content and safe and soft. He didn't want to see her bones anymore, or that look of fear in her eyes when there was an unexpected sound.

"It's been two weeks, little brother. All of her marks are gone, you can quit staring at her."

"Huh?"

Bradley started and looked over his shoulder to see Benji walking up to him, a new tack in his hands. Ah, right. He'd been making himself useful repairing the horse gear that was looking a little long in the tooth. He swore, his brother could about fix anything in a couple of hours.

"You stare at that lady in the same way you stare at your books when you go into that zone of yours. Like you're trying to examine or memorize every part of her. One would think you've had plenty of time to do that in the three whole weeks she's been here, but her face has done quite a bit of changing."

"I like to make sure that she's okay."

"Yeah, because she's in real danger out there with Missy. What are they doing today?"

"Painting, apparently."

Bradley picked up with where he was tending to the horses. Normally he didn't really help with chores unless two or more of his brothers were off doing their own things or sick, but he'd taken to spending the two hours between ten and noon doing things around the barn. And if that happened to give him a front-row view of Missy and Sophia's activities... well, that was a happy coincidence.

"Makes sense. Your girl's an artist, right?"

"Please stop calling her 'my girl.'" Bradley bristled, his brother's amiable nature rubbing him the wrong way.

"Why not, she is, isn't she?"

Bradley almost automatically snapped a "no" but pulled it back just in time. "She's more than that. I don't own her."

"Okay, okay, message received. Dani says that I need to work on my possessive language a bit. Guess this reinforces a bit of her preaching."

"Preaching, huh? I'm not so sure she'd want to hear you call it that."

"Hah, ain't that right? But that's always been my girl. Wait, I... uh, you know what I mean. My... partner?"

Bradley chuckled. "Don't worry about it. I don't think Dani minds being called your girl the way Sophia does."

"That makes sense." Benji sidled up beside him and handed him a chilled water bottle. "You know, for an engaged couple, the two of you don't seem to do much of the, uh, engaging."

"What do you mean?" Bradley asked cautiously. He wasn't

used to lying, and it all seemed so complicated. If his plan hadn't actually worked to get that man and his cop friends away, he would probably regret all of it.

"Well, I know for the first few months together, Dani and I couldn't keep our hands off each other. Got to the point where we couldn't let ourselves be alone after the sun set. But you and Miss Hernandez? I don't think I've seen you so much as hold hands."

"We're private," Bradley said, practically out of habit. "And we find our time when we need it. She's healing from a lot of stuff, so we take things slow."

"Really? Being engaged to a woman you've only known for a few months is slow?"

"Well, that was mostly for her own protection. We both figured out that having someone legally tied to her that wasn't her ex or his folks would be a big help. We were planning on going public with it eventually, once she was comfortable, but that kinda got rushed from the unfortunate visit."

"It sure did, didn't it?" Benji laughed and patted Bradley's back. "You've always had your own way of going about things, haven't you?"

"Yeah, I guess so."

Benji let the subject go at that, dismissing himself to grab some more tack and a saddle. His words made Bradley think, however, and he realized that he should probably do more if he wanted to sell the idea that he and Sophia were a real thing.

He was so involved in his thoughts that he didn't even notice how much time had passed until he heard a gentle cough at the end of the stall he was in. Turning, he was surprised to see Sophia standing there, a picnic basket in the crook of one of her arms and a blanket under the other. She still had bits of paint spattering her hands and even across her nose, but it was all very cute.

"You hungry?" she asked simply, almost looking nervous.

His stomach gave an appreciative growl. "Yeah, I could eat."

"I thought maybe we should eat together. You know, maybe actually act like a couple aside from our once a day ride around the ranch."

"Hey, I like those once a day rides around the ranch."

It could have just been a trick of the light, but he swore that she blushed lightly at that.

"Me too." She nodded her head towards the front doors of the barn. "Yesterday Missy took me to this nice spot on the hill overlooking the pond. I thought that'd be a nice place to go eat."

Bradley almost expected for there to be some sort of trick, but Sophia looked earnest. "By all means, lead the way."

She gave him the tiniest smile before doing exactly that, and they walked together across one of the grazing fields and a hill that did indeed overlook the pond. Once they were there, she laid out the blanket and sat right down as if there wasn't anything unusual about their little exchange.

Bradley sat down across from her, making sure to give her enough space, wondering what was in that basket of hers.

"Your Ma helped me make it," she said matter-of-factly. "But I thought this would be nice."

"Yeah, it is."

There was that flush again, then she was handing him a cold glass bottle of apple cider, a very large sandwich, an apple, and some chips and dip. He had no idea how she'd gotten her hands on junk food if Ma was the one who helped her put the thing together. Benji always had to go into town on his own for junk runs because Ma wouldn't buy it for them.

"There's some deviled eggs in there too," she said, fishing around under some cloths and pulling out some utensils first. "Your ma had me put the plate in the center of these ice packs, kinda like a wall."

"Yeah, that's a classic Ma trick to keep things fresh. The packs are also big enough to make sure that they don't get squashed. Ain't nothing worse than warm, squished deviled eggs."

She chuckled at that. "Well, I could think of a few things."

Bradley felt guilty for a moment at his poor choice of words, but a glimpse of the rueful grin on her face cleared that right up. It was a good sign that she was able to start to joke about things, right? Seemed that way to him.

They slid into silence again as she unpacked two plates and split the food between the two of them. Despite the sandwich loaded with an absolutely delicious amount of roast beef and pepper jack cheese, he decided to start with the veggies. Once those were done, he went to the apple, and then finally, to his sandwich.

It was nice, just sitting there, listening to the breeze cut through the grass and the sounds of the workers at their jobs and the animals making their various noises. He often sat in silence while he worked out numbers in his office, but it was different with Sophia. She didn't seem to expect anything of him. In fact, she seemed to appreciate it when he did nothing.

"How do you do it?" she said.

Bradley blinked, looking up at Sophia with his mouth full. It took him a couple solid seconds to finish chewing and swallow it down.

"Do what?"

"Make me forget."

Bradley stared at her a moment more, trying to figure out if he was being particularly dense. "I don't follow."

She set down her sandwich and gave him a long, earnest look. "You make me forget about all the bad things in my life. Sometimes, in moments like these, all of those things that I know are there, that I know are waiting for me... they kinda... disappear, and it's just me and you. In the moment. *Living.* I'd forgotten what it's like to *live.*"

Of all the things Bradley had expected to come out of her mouth, that was nowhere on the list. He stared at her a long moment before he remembered that he should probably say something back.

"I want you to be safe, Sophia. That's all. If my family and me are making you feel that way, well, I'd consider that a job well done."

"I..." She looked like she was struggling to say something, or perhaps even that she wanted to argue, but instead she nodded and then picked up a deviled egg, popping the thing into her mouth whole. It wasn't until she fully chewed and swallowed that she nodded. "Okay. A job well done. Right."

They fell quiet again, and Bradley picked his sandwich up. But as he did, her words echoed in his head.

All this time he thought that he stressed her out, that his concern for her was too much of a weight and that he needed to give her as much space as he could considering their little engagement ruse. But that didn't seem to be at all the situation. He was making her feel like she was *living*, as she had put it. Even if only for a couple of minutes a day, he was keeping all the bad thoughts away and letting her just exist for a moment. Just breathe without fear or paranoia.

That... that was a heady thought, and it weighed with him long after they packed up the lunch and returned home. But as he went up to his office to work on some new research before dinner and the horse ride, he couldn't help but think that her revelation changed some things.

...or maybe everything.

11

——————

Bradley

For the first time in a long time, Bradley's life felt appropriately full.

It was strange, going from longing for something he didn't understand and denying that anything was missing at all, to suddenly feeling fulfilled without even that much of a shift. But there definitely *was* a shift, because that empty sort of ache hadn't been in his chest in weeks.

It'd been a full month since Sophia joined them and a good two weeks since she even mentioned leaving. Their time together had only increased since their picnic on the hill; either she would come up and eat lunch in his office or ask him to go out to the yard and eat with her. Between supper and their ride, when she used to sit on the porch with Ma, she'd taken to coming up to his office and drawing on her tablet for a while.

It was nice. Bradley found he concentrated even better with her there, the soft scratching of her stylus against her screen, or the sound of her shifting giving him something to ground him to reality when his head started getting away from himself. She also was pretty good about reminding him to drink and eat on a regular schedule, something he hadn't quite managed to do himself in all of his twenty-five years.

Yeah, it was pretty nice, as much as things could be considering the situation, and he was content to pretend to be engaged for a good, long while if this was what it was like.

Of course, he should have known better.

He was alone in his office, a late afternoon, in the middle of researching expanding their brand into organic yogurts and other processed dairy products beyond cheese and milk when his office phone rang shrilly, nearly startling him out of his chair.

It wasn't his personal cell, which meant it had to be business. Collecting himself, he cleared his throat then picked up.

"Bradley Miller, of the Miller Ranch, how may I help you?"

"Hey, yeah, this is Randall down at the police station. Uh, I was calling to ask if you know a Miss Sophia Hernandez?"

Suddenly the entire world shrank down to a single point. Fighting to keep his tone steady, Bradley swallowed. "Yes. She's my fiancé." The lie fell off his tongue more and more easily nowadays. He didn't know quite what that meant, but it certainly wasn't the moment to ponder it.

"Fiancé? Well, I'll be. Y'all Miller boys are getting snatched up all in a row, ain't cha?"

But Bradley wasn't interested in his friendly banter. "You mentioned Sophia. Where is she? Is she alright? Was she attacked? Hurt?"

A dozen and one ideas came to him all at once. He hadn't even known she was in town! As far as he knew, she'd only ever left the property once, and that was with a full escort of all the girls.

"Whoa, whoa. We have her in custody right here. She's fine, for the most part."

"And why was she arrested?"

"I'm not sure, to be honest, I'm not the one on the scene. It says here on her papers disorderly conduct, and I'd believe that from the shiner she gave me."

"She *hit* you?"

He let out a slight chuckle. "It ain't the worst I had. Why don't you come down? It's a bit of a mess here, and I think it would help clear things up. For what it's worth, your lady seemed more scared than angry, but she sure has a mean hook."

"Right. I'll be right there. Don't you touch her."

"Hey, it ain't like that. She's resting right now on a padded cot and secure. I know there's always two sides to a story."

Bradley didn't know what to say to that, so he hung up without responding. Heart in his throat, he rushed down the stairs, racing past anyone in his path and bursting into the garage.

The automated door had never taken so long to rise, but once it did, he was burning rubber to hit the drive. He definitely broke all of the speed limits getting to town, not slowing down until he reached where other cars and people would be. But while he didn't want to endanger anyone's life, he couldn't help but bounce in his seat, wishing that *someone* would go just a *bit* faster.

A thousand and one possibilities were flooding his mind as

to what happened. He was piecing what little info he had together like a puzzle, hoping and praying that Sophia was alright.

So, she had gone into town without letting him know. Not that she needed his permission or anything, but she always let him know when she was deviating from her schedule of her own accord. That was odd.

Also, arrested for disorderly conduct, but not assault. So the cop she'd punched in the eye apparently wasn't interested in pressing charges. That boded well but... still. She was in *jail*. Or at least a holding cell. He didn't know what to think about that.

Had she been set off? Was this more of her ex's doing? Or had she had a sudden panic attack? A psychotic break? Did someone startle her and she decked them on accident?

So many questions, not enough info. He *knew* Sophia wasn't the type to just randomly cause mayhem for no reason, so the question was, what set her off?

He was no closer to having any answers by the time he pulled into the lot in front of the small sheriff's office and jail. He knew that things were more complicated in big cities, but he was quite grateful for once at the simplicity of living on the edge of a small town.

He stormed in through the door, banging it against the wall as he strode in. Sure enough, one of the officers with what looked like a growing black eye stood up from behind one of the desks.

"Hey there," he said, standing up with a friendly grin. "I take it you're the young Bradley Miller? I think out of all the boys, I see you the least. Hardly even knew what you looked like."

"I tend to stay around the ranch," Bradley answered firmly. "Where's Sophia?"

"Right this way. We've been keeping her in the back. Come on."

He picked up a set of keys from behind the desk and walked off. Bradley followed after, so many emotions churning through him that he thought he might combust right then and there.

Eventually, they did make it to a couple of large holding cells that were all empty. Except for one, where Sophia was laying down on a cot.

"Sophia!" he cried out automatically, rushing to the bars. She didn't respond, however, her breathing steady and even. "Sophia! Wake up!"

She didn't even budge, and he rounded on the cop. "What's going on?"

"Well, like I said, she was putting up quite a fight when we got her in here. Almost like a frenzy. We had to sedate her for her own good."

"You had to... sedate... her," Bradley repeated. In all his life, he could remember losing his temper a grand total of twice before he hit twenty-five. But he could feel that he was about to lose it again, his anger ramping up hot and fast. "Did you ever think that maybe she was panicking because you brought her to a *police station*? This is exactly where her ex has the best access to her!"

"Her ex? Uh, pardon me, Mr. Miller, sir, but I feel like I'm missing out on part of the story here."

"All you need to know is being here is bad for her. I'll be taking her home now."

"Hold up now, sir. We need you to sign some papers. Now the grocery isn't really keen on pressing charges, but she went nuts in there and started knocking over shelves, screaming and causing a scene. Are you sure your lady might not need some professional help?"

"I mean, maybe she *could* use a therapist," Bradley hesitantly replied. He had nothing against them. Bart saw one on the regular. "But that's disconnected from whatever this business is. Sophia wouldn't have just randomly 'gone crazy.' Something, or most likely someone, was threatening her."

"Uh, look, sir. I know you're out to protect her, but we don't have any reports—"

There was a thundering bang, and Bradley realized it was the front door being slammed open much as he had entered.

"Gosh dang it, I told the sheriff we need to put one of them door stopper things before the townsfolk bust the handle right through the wall. This'll have to wait a second. I can't leave you back here."

Bradley wanted to argue, but he knew it wouldn't get him anywhere, so he angrily followed after the officer as they headed back to the front.

But surprisingly enough, it was Chastity and Missy who had busted in, both of them breathing hard and looking around wildly.

"What were you two thinking?!" he heard himself shout before he even really thought it through. "You took Sophia into town, and she ends up in jail?"

"I'm sorry!" Chastity took a deep breath, her face flushed and sweat was all across her brow. "It was her ex. We were just walking along, shopping for this surprise meal she wanted to make the family, when suddenly he was right there. He's *big*, Bradley. *Real* big."

"I had Chastity run to the front while I pulled out my

phone to call the cops," Missy cut in. "But he grabbed it and stomped on it right there in front of me. I slugged him one, but... man, that guy is a *tank*. He basically *threw* me and then managed to corner Sophia before I could get back on my feet."

The blond grinned. "You should have seen her, though. She really stood up for herself. She screamed at him that she wasn't going to listen to him anymore and that her fiancé was gonna be mad he was there bothering her. He said that he didn't see any sort of ring, so she just up and pushed a shelf over on him! It was *something*.

"By that point, me n' Chastity got back to her to check if she was alright. She was shaking real hard but seemed to be okay, so we went to make sure her ex stuck around to get his just desserts this time, but he had already pushed the shelf up and was running out the door. We went after him on instinct, but we lost him. When we went back to the grocery store, Sophia was gone. We've been running around like crazy trying to figure out what happened!"

Bradley stood there a moment, digesting it all. The puzzle in his head started to come together, snapping into place like a clear picture.

"I have a pretty good idea." He looked to the officer, who certainly looked surprised by the recent developments. "Who called the cops, and were they there when you got to the scene?"

"Uh, let me check the notes. The arresting officers got called back out again." He crossed to the same desk that he had been sitting at when Bradley entered. "Uh, it looks here like it was an older gentleman, big, with salt and pepper hair. First name Jack, uh, last name... uh, it doesn't say."

Bradley could be wrong, but that sounded exactly like the

ex's father. He wished that he could say he was surprised, but he wasn't at all.

But he was concerned. It was clear that his engagement ruse wasn't enough. Or at least that he wasn't putting nearly enough effort into it. No ring, of course the son of a cop would notice that right off the bat.

If he wanted Sophia to stay with his family, or just to be safe and happy in general, he needed to do a better job of protecting her.

He *had* to.

"I'll be taking Sophia now," he said. "She needs to go home."

"Wait, there's just one more thing. While the grocery isn't one to press charges, they are a bit concerned about all the damages. They wanted to know if she would be willing to pay for some of what was lost."

"Fine," Bradley said. "Whatever they said, I'll write you a check right now."

"Oh, uh, are you certain, sir? I thought you might want to talk to one of your lawyers."

"No. I want this done and over with. Tell me the amount."

He did, and Bradley went back to his truck, pulling his checkbook from his glove compartment. He had plenty of money saved up from working all the time, never leaving the ranch and his own investments in his personal portfolio, so he didn't care what the grocery wanted. He just needed Sophia to be safe. And she certainly wasn't safe where she was.

Thankfully, the whole process went quickly, and soon he was being walked back to where they were holding Sophia.

"You're not the one who sedated her, were you?" he asked.

"Me? Oh no. Guns, bar fights and the like I'm all good for, but I don't do needles. No, it was our medic that did her up."

"You have a medic?"

"Yeah. She's a real sweet lady. Works with the people we have in the jail who are waiting to be shipped out to the state penitentiary. Or the drunks in the tank. So don't worry, she did the best she could for your girl."

"The best thing for my girl would be never being brought here in the first place. She's the victim in all this, but she ended up being the one arrested!"

"Yeah, I'm really sorry about that, sir. I'll make sure that everyone in the precinct knows to look out for these fellers who are trying to abuse their authority."

"Yeah, you do that."

The officer opened the door for him, and Bradley went in. Sophia's eyes fluttered slightly as he approached, but she stayed soundly asleep.

Oh well, maybe that would make this easier for her. He hated the thought of her sitting in the jail, waiting for him to arrive, wondering if her ex was going to make it there first.

Crouching in front of her, he scooped her up in his arms and against his chest. She was lighter than she should have been, but not as badly as she had been when they had first met. When he stood, he noticed bandages around her wrist with a slight bit of dark brown seeping through them.

"What's this?" he asked sharply.

"Like I said, she was hurting herself. The arresting officer put her in handcuffs, and she fought 'em really hard. The medic was worried if she broke the skin much further that she'd hit a vein or damage a nerve. That's what started the whole sedation decision."

Bradley bit back exactly what he wanted to say to that and headed out the front doors. Missy and Chastity accompanied him on either side, quiet and grim.

Once more, all of them had underestimated exactly what Sophia had told them. Her ex really was relentless, and it was terrifying. All this time, Bradley thought he was doing right by her, but it wasn't nearly enough.

Not at all.

"You two go back to your car and ride home. I'll come after you, but I'll be going slower. I don't want to jostle Sophia."

"Right. You gonna be okay, Bradley?" Chastity asked, a comforting hand on his arm.

"Right now, I'm not the one I'm worried about."

"I know. But you matter too, in all this. I know you like to act all logical and like you're not as sappy as the rest of us, but I see how much she means to you."

"Just head home. Let them know what happened. We're going to need to come up with a plan to handle this."

"Okay, Bradley. We'll see you at home."

The two women headed off, leaving Bradley to put Sophia in his passenger seat and buckle her up. Finally, he was able to look her fully over, and he felt so guilty. Her forehead was covered in sweat, and it looked like there was a scratch on her chin. There were the bandages around her wrist, and he was sure that when her eyes opened that they would be bloodshot.

Couldn't life just give her a *little* bit of a break?

It seemed not.

Shaking his head, he closed the door and went over to his side of the truck. Pulling out, he resolved to do a better job in making Sophia safe.

The kind of job she deserved.

12

———

Sophia

*S*ophia's head felt like cotton.

No... her head felt like it was an empty helium balloon that had been filled up and let go too many times, and *then* stuffed with cotton.

Wait, that didn't make sense either.

Why were all of her thoughts so groggy? The last thing she remembered was walking around the grocery store. In her downtime between lessons with Missy and drawing commissions, she'd taken to researching different recipes now that she had access to food. She wanted to do something special for the Millers, so she'd asked Missy and Chastity to take her into town. And also sworn them to secrecy.

But then, her ex—

Her ex!

Sophia sat up with a jolt, throwing herself to the side. She was moving, far too fast to be carried, so that meant that she was in a car.

"Let me go!" she screamed, bringing up her fists like Missy had taught her and twisting so that she could kick at the driver.

"Whoa, whoa, Sophia, it's me! You're alright, it's okay. I got you. Your ex ran off again."

The voice. Sophia knew that voice. That voice meant that she was safe.

"Bradley?" she asked hazily, her vision clearing.

"Yeah. Sophia, it's me. It's okay, you're in my truck and we're headed home."

"Home."

She sat up slowly, her heartbeat coming down. Her ex... her ex had been at the grocery, but she wasn't at the grocery. She was safe.

But why was her head so... *funny*?

She didn't know, but more and more of her memory slid back to her. Cops had shown up and she'd tried to tell them what happened, but they'd treated her like *she* was the bad one. The next thing she knew, cuffs were being put on her, and she was being dragged.

She'd yelled at them that they had everything all messed up, yeah, but she'd managed to keep mostly calm until she thought she saw a glimpse of her ex's father outside one of the windows. Then everything had clicked together, and she understood that this was a setup. Even if she didn't go with *him*, there was a backup plan to get her to where they could easily load her up and haul her out.

And that... that was so *terrifying*.

Even with the fake engagement, even with all the Millers on

her side, they still wouldn't stop. Would they ever stop? Or was she going to have to lay in the ground, cold and dead, before they finally would leave her be?

But then, right when her mind was done wrapping itself around that, the embarrassment set in.

She was pretty sure that she had been passed out, which wasn't great. But she had also been in literal *jail* before that, which meant that Bradley had bailed her out. How humiliating! His family was helping her out, letting her stay with them for free, and she repaid them by getting arrested and costing them *more* money? And what would she do when she had to show up for court? When even was her court date? And would *he* be there?

One thing for certain was that Bradley had to hate her now. He had been so kind, so patient, and she'd thrown all of that back in his face.

She surely hadn't meant to. She was just trying to do something nice for the family. To show them how much she appreciated all of them. But she's messed that up too.

She could hear her breath picking up into a wheeze, and her heart was beating hard again like it was trying to break through her rib cage.

"Hey, easy there. You're safe, okay? I promise. We're on the ranch property, almost to the house."

"I'm sorry," she gasped, barely able to get the words out.

"Hey, hey, there's nothing to be sorry about. Hold on, let me pull over and we can talk. Just breathe for me in the meantime, okay? In and out."

He was being so nice again, but it made it sting more. She'd messed up. And she knew she was too broken for someone like him.

They pulled off the road and up to a cluster of oaks. The sun was almost done setting, leaving a thin line of burning viridian across the skyline.

They came to a stop, and she watched Bradley put the truck into park then pull up the emergency brake. Oh no, this was probably the part where he told her she would have to go soon. Where he told her that she was too much for his family, that she had caused one too many problems.

"Hey, are you alright?" he asked, turning to look at her with concern across his features.

"I'm fine. I'm sorry. I just—"

"Hey, I told you that you didn't need to apologize. I know that your ex was involved in this whole fiasco. None of it was your fault." He reached out tentatively as if he was going to stroke her face, but he stopped himself before he made contact. "Look, I'm sorry that I wasn't there to protect you. That I wasn't enough."

No, no, no. He was plenty enough. Too many of his words sounded like sweet but empty comforts someone said before delivering bad news. He was going to tell her it was time for her to leave.

But that couldn't happen. She finally had found a place with the Millers, and she was so close to having several grand saved up. If she was frugal with it, she'd be able to live decent for about a year.

Besides, she liked Ma, Chastity, Missy, Dani, and all the rest. They were fun. And they felt like real friends. Not to mention Bradley. She liked the quiet in her head when she was around him. The serenity he brought her. She even liked the strange feeling in her chest that she got every so often when she looked at him.

The Millers were the only ones who ever believed her, who had ever tried to keep her ex away, and she couldn't lose that. She *had* to make him like her again. Make him look at her like he did during that first picnic.

But what to do? Like *he* had said, she was more trouble than she was worth and not particularly good at much. She wasn't smart and had a knack for giving people headaches. Her ex had always said if it weren't for her pretty face, she wouldn't be worth much at all.

But that was fine. She could use that.

She didn't have a choice.

13

———

Bradley

*B*radley looked up at the night sky for a moment, trying to contain his anger at Sophia's ex. The fearful look in her mismatched eyes, the pale tint to her normally golden skin, she looked like a woman who was truly haunted, and he *hated* it.

He wanted to wipe that look away. To make it so she never knew fear again, but that monster of a man was ruining it!

Still, it would do Sophia no good for him to lose his temper. She'd probably just internalize it as anger at her, and that was the last thing he wanted. He was sure that the sedative they injected her with wasn't helping. He could tell by her slightly slurred words and added confusion to everything that she still wasn't feeling like her normal self.

"Hey, let's just sit for a minute. Breathe a little. You wanna listen to some music?"

She nodded, her face looking screwed up in concentration. But as he went to turn on the radio, she caught his hand, pulling it to gently touch her face.

Bradley was surprised, that was for certain. It was the most intimate moment that they'd ever shared, and she was the one who had initiated it. He went with it, however, his thumb stroking away the tear tracks on her cheek.

He hated that her ex was still making her cry. He wanted to soothe her, to protect her, to keep her safe until every cell in her body knew she didn't have to be afraid anymore.

He could stay in that moment forever, just touching her face, comforting her, but then suddenly she was moving, crawling into his lap and kissing him.

Now *that* was a shock. A shock that went right through his system, jolting his brain so that his body reacted before his mind did.

It was so easy to sink into the kiss. She was so warm, so soft atop him, even with some of her bones sticking out a little more than they should on her frame. She smelled like pomegranate, and the weight of her made his blood rush in a way he hadn't felt in a long time.

A *real* long time.

His hands went around her back and he pulled her to him. She let out the slightest of whimpers, wrapping her arms around his neck, but it was that uncertain sound that brought him back to reality.

The kiss felt good, that was for certain, but it wasn't right.

Like a wrecking ball, his practical side swung in, shattering the haze of pure *want* that had filled him and making him realize exactly what was going on.

"Wait," he breathed headily, breaking away and pushing her back a little. It was an awkward balance, with both of her slender yet muscled legs on either side of his own thighs and the steering wheel behind her, but he kept one hand on her back to steady her.

Her eyes went wide at that, however, and she leaned in almost determinedly, kissing him with twice the ferocity.

"Sophia, I said *wait*."

It took much more willpower than he would like to admit for him to lift her up and put her back in the seat next to him, turning and putting an arm up to keep her from crowding him again.

She looked up at him a moment, just a moment, desperate and begging and oh, so beautiful, before his words sank in and she broke into outright sobs.

"Please, don't get rid of me. I can be good, I promise." Suddenly she was up on her knees, both of her hands gripping his arm as she leaned in as close as he would let her. Tears were flowing freely down her face, and he didn't think that he'd ever seen something so heartbreaking. "I can be real good to you, I promise. Just don't make me leave, okay? Don't, *please*?"

He thought her expression was heartbreaking, but the words out of her mouth made his heart outright shatter. With slow and careful movements, he took her hands in his own and made sure she looked him in the eye as he spoke.

"Listen, I need you to understand what I'm about to say, okay?"

"Anything, please, just don't make me leave yet."

Like he ever could. "Sophia, you never, *ever* have to try to earn your keep with us, you get that? Not with your money, not with your time, and especially not with your—" He faltered a moment but forced himself to push through. "Not with your body either, okay? If you want to freeload in the main house until you're ninety, that's fine with me. That's fine with everyone in the whole family. You have a place with us, no conditions, no fine print, no paying back. It's an open invitation, you got that?"

"... no one is that nice," she whispered, squeezing her eyes shut. "No one gives everything for nothing."

Bradley didn't know how to respond to that. He wanted to tell her that she was wrong, but she'd lived such a different life than him. Maybe he was the one in the bubble.

"I guess my brothers did say that I've always been different."

She didn't answer that and just sat there, her sniffles slowing. He reached into his glove box and pulled out some tissues he'd stashed in there last time he had a summer cold and handed her a few.

Once it seemed like she mostly settled, he held up the plastic bag he kept in the back for trash. "You ready to go back to the main house? Maybe have a good lie down and sleep off the rest of those sedatives, huh?"

But she just shook her head. "No. Not really. Can you... can you maybe just... hold me?" She must have felt him hesitate because she rushed to continue. "Just, like a friend would. Like Missy."

He smiled at that. "Missy has always been a touchy one. Yeah, I can do that. Come'ere."

"Thank you."

A little shakily, she curled into his side. He hated the circumstances that lead them up to that point, but she felt *right* sitting against him.

With one arm, he cracked the windows open and turned the truck off. Leaning the seat back, he settled down to look at the stars with Sophia beside him. Right where he could protect her.

And it was in his truck, looking up at the beautiful night sky, that he held her while she slept.

14

———————

Sophia

Sophia was pretty sure that she was in love.

Which was stupid and silly and impossible and irresponsible and...and... and a whole lot of other things, but that didn't stop it from being what it was. Ever since that moment in Bradley's car, when she threw herself at him to distract him from hating her, from hurting her, just like her ex and he had turned her down.

Strange, that it was rejection that solidified her feelings for him, but it was exactly what she needed. When she was at her weakest, her most vulnerable, offering herself up willingly to him under the influence of the sedatives, he hadn't been willing to take the bait. Somehow, he knew that her motives came from a dark, sticky place that always whispered how worthless she was. How she could only buy favor for a time until her presence outweighed her usefulness.

Her ex had never done that. No, he'd pressured her into being intimate after just a few months of dating. She hadn't been ready. She'd been scared and nervous, but she had been so afraid of losing him, so she'd let him go further and further, until suddenly she was in a situation where she felt like she couldn't back out. If he'd noticed her trepidation, he certainly didn't say so, and that had been that.

From then on, when things started to go bad, she learned that she could sometimes distract her ex from his anger with a good kiss, or even taking off her top. Sometimes that didn't work at all, though. And sometimes he demanded her body even when she wasn't in the mood.

So for her, intimacy had always been a bargaining chip. Not something to be shared between two people in love.

But Bradley wasn't interested in that kind of transaction.

In fact, he didn't demand *any* transaction. And every time she thought about that, she got a strange, floaty feeling that made her feel like she could head right up to the clouds.

They ate every lunch together up in his office, except he stopped working on his numbers during the hour break, and instead they would sit and talk. She learned so much about him, from the fact that he was in drama club and had been Judd in *Oklahoma, to* during his freshman year he'd read a book a day from his school's library.

If anyone missed them at lunch, no one said anything, which was saying something for the Miller family.

And perhaps most exciting of them all, a week after the incident with her ex, Bradley had announced that she was good enough with Hyacinth to ride without him guiding her and that he was going to ride beside her on one of his own mounts.

So their evening walks turned into evening trots, and there was nothing compared to the feeling of roving all over the ranch with him, on horses side by side. Sometimes his gelding grew frustrated with Sophia's much tamer pace, but Bradley would urge the beast to run in broad circles until he calmed down.

It was magic, pure magic, and she found herself more content than she ever had been. Sure, she wasn't confessing her love for Bradley. In fact, she was fine with keeping her feelings to herself for the rest of eternity, all safe and exciting in her chest. She hadn't been in love since she was seventeen, and that had all turned out to be a trick, so she was more than happy to sit in the experience and wait it out.

But all of that changed by the two-week mark after the moment in the truck.

She'd had no warning that anything was going to shift. But like all big things, it happened in a moment.

She was sitting beside Bradley on the comfy couch in his office, legs tucked under her as she sketched, and he ate. Suddenly, he stood up, knocking her concentration.

"Oh, I uh, got something for you. If you want it. I... I thought it might be useful."

His nervous demeanor made her curious. There was a lot of things that Bradley was, but shy wasn't exactly one of them. The man crossed over to his desk and opened one of the drawers, pulling out a small, white box. Returning to her, he set it on the table.

"What is it?"

"Open it and find out."

Sophia looked from him to the box and back. Despite living with the generous Millers for a little over a month and a half, she'd managed to avoid any direct gifts from them. Somehow it seemed like too much on top of all the other amazing things they did for her.

But still, how could she tell him no?

Tentatively, she reached out for the box, drawing it to her with slightly trembling hands. It wasn't wrapped fancily, just a regular box. All she had to do was slide the case out of the paper thingy and pop it open.

There were a lot of things she was wondering if it could be, but the last thing she expected was a beautiful ring sitting right in a little satin pillow.

"W-what?" she sputtered, heart stilling in her chest. It was a silver band—or was it white gold—inlaid with several small jewels in a row. It was exactly her style, and she wondered when she had ever mentioned that she hated diamonds to Bradley. "I don't understand, what is this for?" Her mind was kicking off in a flurry of thoughts. Did he feel the same way that she did? It certainly seemed like quite the jump, and she wasn't sure that she was ready for it, but—

"Missy said that your ex noticed you had no ring, so I thought this would help us sell the story better. We need people to believe us if I'm gonna keep you safe."

Oh.

Right.

Disappointment came crashing in on her, but that made no sense. She *knew* that their engagement was fake. All of it was fake. Bradley didn't feel romantically inclined towards her at all, he was just doing this out of the goodness of his heart. He was a kind, wonderful protector. He was a good man.

And good men didn't fall in love with women like her.

"It's beautiful," she managed to squeak out. "Thank you. So much."

"Of course," he answered, sounding quite relieved. "I was worried it would make you uncomfortable."

"No, not uncomfortable, don't worry about that. This was very thoughtful of you."

It wasn't a lie. She wasn't uncomfortable in the slightest.

Just maybe a little brokenhearted.

15

———————

Bradley

"So what are we doing now?" Sophia asked, looking out of the window of his truck as they cruised along.

"Something I thought you might like, maybe get more word going about us, start up some town gossip."

She laughed and looked over to him. "Oh, so this isn't just because you wanted to hang out with me?"

"Who *wouldn't* want to hang out with you?" he said playfully.

It was amazing. Ever since their incident in the truck, things had shifted between him and Sophia. She didn't seem remotely scared of him and was more open with him than she had ever been. Sure, sometimes she was still sad, and she still jumped when startled, but she didn't seem nearly as on edge as she was before she fell asleep in his arms under the stars.

He wasn't naïve enough to think that she was magically fixed. No, she needed a lot more healing and counseling for that. But it was nice to not have to worry if she was going to break into a thousand pieces at any moment.

And as for her ex and his father, they hadn't made a move since the whole grocery incident. Apparently, the cops had put the word out about the two of 'em, and the last of their supposed 'connections' had dried up.

Good.

Personally, Bradley would prefer if they were straight up arrested, but apparently Sophia still didn't want to press charges, and he wasn't going to push her. Not yet, at least. That was her decision for her to face when she knew that she was strong enough.

"I am excited to be out with you."

Bradley shot her a quick look over his arm that was gripping the steering wheel. "Did you just say you were happy to be out of the house in public?"

"Yeah. I think I just did. With you, anyway."

Bradley laughed again, reveling in the moment. "Huh, times really are a'changin' aren't they?"

"Maybe a little. I mean, I am in a dress, after all. Missy said I *had* to dress up."

Yeah, she definitely *was* in a dress. While all of his older brothers were either into curvier or larger ladies, he liked a much broader range. Small, waifish kind of women with big eyes and slender fingers, chubby women who were soft and warm and comforting in their weight. Tall and statuesque, small and curvy, and also fit and muscular like an amazon.

Sophia was somewhere right between slim and athletic, with nearly two months with his family allowing for her bones to disappear back into her body where they belonged and her muscles to become more prominent. Of course, considering that all of her clothes seemed to be oversized and baggy, as if their purpose was to hide her body, it certainly was a shock to see her in a formfitting, bright blue dress that Missy had ordered online for her.

It wasn't so tight that it was indecent, but it flattered her feminine form in a way that *really* tested Bradley's desire not to ogle the woman. Even sitting there in the passenger's seat of his truck, her legs tucked up under her and her high-heeled shoes on the floor, she was a vision.

She was wearing makeup too, and it was clear that Chasity had done her hair. She mostly always wore it up in a loose bun, or in a ponytail. But today it was in a beautiful braid that must've taken a while to do. Strands of hair were wisping around her face and neck and Bradley thought she looked amazing.

It was easy to forget that the whole arrangement was fake. He wanted to whisk her away so he could bask in her presence. But he got the feeling that anything like that would make Sophia uncomfortable, so if he had to dress it up as a part of the 'plan' so he could spoil her, well then, he would do just that.

"You never answered my question, you know."

"Oh, I didn't? Well then, I'm taking you to one of the most popular restaurants in the city. With lots of people and good security, and great food."

"Wait, in the city? That doesn't sound like a good way to get people here to talk about us."

"Trust me, there's always someone from town there. When I say it's popular, I mean *popular*."

"Well then," she said nervously. "I guess we can try it out."

But he heard the slight tremor in her voice. "We don't have to, if you don't want to."

"No, it's okay. I want to try. I think... I think maybe my ex has been scared off for a while after I pushed an entire shelf over on him. I've never raised my hand against him before."

"I'd like to do a lot more than just raise my hand to him..." Bradley grumbled. Thankfully, that didn't seem to make her uncomfortable, and she just sighed wistfully.

"Wishes, wishes, as slippery as fishes."

"What was that?"

"Nothing. Just something my mother used to say." She heaved a sigh. "Do you think I should try to reach out to her? We haven't talked in... too long."

"Yeah, I don't see why not. I know you kept your distance for both your and their safety for a while, but since you're safe here with us, seems like an appropriate time."

"What would I even say?"

As good as Bradley was with numbers, he still wasn't that great with this kind of stuff. "I'm not sure, to be honest. I'd start with saying that you were safe and go from there."

"Yeah... safe..."

The conversation faded, as it often did with them, and they slid into a comfortable silence. His family members still often commented about how they didn't seem to talk much, but Bradley knew they just didn't understand because it was different than their own relationships. There was something comforting about sitting in her presence, being in the moment with nothing before or after it. They didn't need to have a long, drawn-out conversation. They didn't need to have a movie playing, or always be on some adventure. They could just... *be*.

And that was nice.

They chatted idly a couple more times in the hour it took to reach the city, but mostly it was just the serene quiet. Bradley had never felt so at home with someone who wasn't family, and by the time he was parking his truck in a lot that cost *way* too much for his car to just sit there for a couple of hours, he was feeling warm and content.

"So, are you gonna actually let me open the door for you this time?"

Sophia paused right in the middle of reaching for the handle, both of her small feet already in her heels. "Oh, uh, right. That's a thing, isn't it?"

"It is for me," he said with a rueful smile.

For the first time since he met her, she stayed put and allowed him to get out and go around the car. He did indeed open her door with a flourish, making a grand gesture as he did.

"This way, my lady."

"Ew, gross. Enough of that."

"What, are you objecting to my obvious charm?"

"I'm objecting to your *fake* charm. We're already in a fake engagement. That's enough duplicity for me."

"Ah, sorry for dragging you into my life of dishonesty. I'd hate to think I was besmirching your honor."

As predicted, she playfully jostled his arm. Despite the kiss they shared—the kiss that kept him up some nights and occupied his dreams far too often—they were still cautious about any sort of physical contact.

Sophia, for obvious reasons. And while it wasn't that

Bradley didn't think he couldn't control himself; he didn't want to dangle that temptation in front of himself. Because when he thought back to Sophia in his lap, all soft and kissing on him, well… it certainly wasn't easy to keep his thoughts church-like.

Besides, it felt like anything physical from her would be taking advantage. It was clear that Sophia felt that she owed him, and he was worried that she still might not understand that she didn't have to use affection or her body, or anything to pay him back. To keep him interested.

"Shouldn't I hold onto your arm or something? You know, to sell the bit?"

Bradley blinked at her for the faintest of seconds, trying to come up with an excuse. "Yeah, that makes sense."

He offered her his arm and both of hers wrapped around it, pulling her close to his side. Instantly his body reacted, all of his senses seeming to jump to high alert. He could feel the heat of her almost acutely through the getup she was wearing, and his nose was filled with the scent of pomegranate and citrus. He felt a bit like a schoolboy, jolted at the sight of the prettiest girl in his class, but he did his best to cover it with a cough.

Thankfully, it wasn't that far of a walk around the building and into the restaurant. Of course, he'd gotten a reservation all the way back when she'd accepted his ring, so they were ushered right to a nice table in the back.

It wasn't a booth, but the restaurant didn't have any. It wasn't *quite* fancy, but it wasn't a chain restaurant either. It was a nice, in-between place that was just high end enough to make it an impressive date night or perfect celebration dinner after an important event.

Sophia seemed reluctant to let go of his arm when they were seated, however, and that stuck in his mind. Sometimes…

well, sometimes with her it seemed like maybe she wasn't pretending.

But that was ridiculous.

Sophia was a beautiful, creative, and talented woman. She had survived things that most people would never even face, and she could still smile. Still laugh. She'd been used and abused and betrayed. All of that meant that her ability to express or interpret affection was twisted around and upside down. So if it seemed like she was looking at him like someone might look at their actual fiancé, it was only because she was feeling grateful. And if it seemed like she didn't shy away from contact with him, or maybe even seek it out, that was just her healing a little.

It wasn't about him, and it would be wrong of him to interpret it that way.

Even if it was really, really tempting.

"So, do you have any recommendations?" Sophia said, picking up the menu and looking it over. Almost instantly a frown settled on her face.

"What?" he asked quickly, his heart skipping a beat. Was there something on there that reminded her of her ex?

"I just... it's really expensive."

Bradley frowned and looked at the menu himself. Sure, it wasn't fast food prices, but most of the stuff was between twenty and forty dollars. Certainly nothing that would completely bust the budget.

"It's fine. Don't worry about it."

She nodded and looked at the menu again before quickly setting it down. "I can't. I just... can't. Can you order something for me?"

He looked uncertainly from the menu to her. "You sure?"

"Yeah, I trust you."

She said them so casually, but those words hit him like an arrow right in the center of his chest.

She... *trusted* him.

After everything she'd been through, all the terrible things she'd seen, all the worst of humanity she'd experienced.

And she trusted *him.*

That was... that was something else. He stared at her for perhaps a bit too long before swallowing and giving her a nod.

The moment seemed to shift gravity right out from under him, but she acted like nothing had happened. And for her, maybe it hadn't. Maybe she said it without thinking. But Bradley knew he was going to lay awake at night replaying the moment, turning it this way and that.

Eventually, however, the waiter came to take their drink order. Bradley went ahead and took the liberty of getting them an appetizer and putting in their meals.

Unfortunately, that left just him and Sophia, and he had no idea what to say to her now.

"So..." he started, rubbing the back of his neck.

"Your hair is getting a little long, you know," she said suddenly.

"Wait, what?"

She laughed, and the tension in him broke. "Sorry, it just felt weird, and I had no idea what to say so I just blurted the first thing that came to my mind."

"And your first thought was that my hair is too long?"

She shrugged. "Well, I know your brother Benji has been growing it his out because Dani likes to run her fingers through it when they're kissing."

If Bradley had just drank anything, he would have spit out

all the liquid in his mouth. "One, please don't ever tell me anything like that about my brothers again. Secondly, how do you even know that?"

Her eyes twinkled as she leaned her chin against her fist. "What, you boys don't gossip together about your romantic lives?"

"What? No. Mostly it's the older trio talking about how wonderful and perfect their ladies are. Or how they accidentally made one of them mad."

"Huh," Sophia said smirking. "We talk about much more than that."

Bradley shifted uncomfortably. "How much more?"

"Not *that* much," she said, catching his meaning. "They keep it decent. But Chastity just likes to gush about how good a kisser Ben is, and Dani is always going on about how Benji can—"

"Alright, again, I ask that you observe rule number one that I just stated."

She laughed gently.

"I just like to see you turn red."

"Ah, this is a new side of you I haven't seen before. I think I like it." He winked at her.

This time they both shared a laugh and settled into a comfortable conversation about Hyacinth and Sophia's goals for the next month. It pleased him that Sophia was planning more long-term. He felt like the first month of her stay she'd always been talking about where she was going next, or how she needed to save up more so she could move on.

As far as he could tell, she was taking commissions steadily. She had to have plenty saved up for a ticket. Maybe even a couple. And for hotel rooms, food, and other supplies. And yet, she was still around.

That made him feel good. She wasn't staying because she thought she had no choice. She was *choosing* to.

And that meant a lot.

Eventually their food did come, but he hardly noticed it. It was good, sure, but to him, Sophia was the star of the show. The conversation fell off while they consumed the two steaks and potatoes in front of them, but the parade of blissed out expressions marching across her face was more than worth it.

They didn't linger long after that. When he noticed Sophia's gaze starting to flit around anxiously, and her shoulders hunch in on herself, he knew it was time to return. Even if he wanted to stay there for hours longer, what he wanted wasn't important.

He left a hundred on the table, not really willing to wait for the server to give them the bill, and stood, offering Sophia his arm. She took it with a soft smile, and then they headed out into the night.

Once more, they were quiet. Enjoying the short stroll together. When they reached the car, he was pleased when she didn't immediately go for the door, instead standing there and looking at him expectantly.

Now that he could work with.

Disentangling himself from her arm, he stepped forward to open the door for her, ready to turn back and give an over-the-top bow, but he was surprised when Sophia was right *there*, only a scant few inches from him and looking up at his face like she was searching for something.

"This was nice," she breathed, a tentative smile pulling at

the corner of her full lips. Lips that were painted such a pretty plum.

Bradley wanted to reach up and gently run this thumb across the color, to feel the softness that he knew was there, the silky skin that kept coming back to him again and again.

But he didn't move. Not even as her breath ghosted over his face and his heart thundered in his ears. He wanted to... he *wanted*—but he couldn't. It wasn't right to want. Not when Sophia had been through so much and he was one of the people providing for her. It was a power imbalance, and he wasn't going to take advantage.

She stayed there a moment, just looking at him, seeming to try to find something but he had no idea what. It took every bit of his willpower not to close the distance between them and sweep her up off her feet.

"Thank you," she said finally, moving past him to get into the truck.

Finally, Bradley could breathe again, and he shut the truck door before going around. Whatever was going on with him, he needed to get it under control. It was clear that he was viscerally attracted to Sophia, but that didn't mean he could go around misconstruing her innocent actions as romance.

He would never be *that* guy.

Once inside, he turned on the radio, a soft indie blues tune playing over it. Sophia curled up in her seat, once more kicking off her heels. She looked contented and happy, like that strange exchange at the door never happened, so he was willing to dismiss it too.

And just like that, they drove home together.

16

———————

Bradley

$\mathscr{B}$radley needed to come to terms with a few things.

First of all, that there were apparently a couple of things that were more important to him than the accounting on the ranch and protecting his family's prosperity.

Secondly, that he enjoyed having company much more than he thought he did, and it wasn't nearly as tiring as he once would have considered it.

And thirdly, he was most definitely in love with Sophia.

He tried to fight it, he really did, but after another two weeks of bliss, two weeks of no ex, no ex's father, no bumps or bruises, it was impossible to ignore. Everything about Sophia called out to him in the best ways possible.

It was little things, to how she chewed her lip when she drew on her tablet, or how she trusted Missy to cut her hair back down to a short, more manageable do that framed her high cheekbones nicely. To how she bought a present for Benji's birthday although no one expected her to. There was the way her tongue would stick out of the corner of her mouth as she stirred pancake batter for Ma, and how she would baby talk to all the animals, no matter how huge or tall they were.

And there were big things too. Like how she took to life on the ranch like a duck to water. The chickens loved her especially, for some reason, and she was the only one aside from Missy and one of his little cousins who never got pecked.

And also, how one day, she came up to the office all serious and without her tablet. At first he'd been alarmed when she sat down in front of his desk—the couch was always her go-to. But then she'd cleared her throat and asked him about getting health insurance since she was going to be around a while.

The thought that she was willing to stick around long enough for health insurance to be needed had nearly made him giddy right then and there. But then she had gone on to say that it was time she saw a therapist so she could move on and find out who she really was, and it took a whole lot of acting experience not to show how beside himself he was with happiness.

Therapy was a *huge* deal. He'd thought that some counseling would do Sophia wonders, and maybe even a support group of other women who'd been through what she had, but he was never sure if she was ready. The fact that she'd brought it up all on her own? *Amazing.*

And that she'd gone to her first appointment with Dani and Keiko in tow *and* had scheduled one a week for the next month?

Well, Bradley didn't have a word for it, but it sure did feel good in his soul.

Because the woman he loved was healing. Slowly but surely, all the cracks that had formed were filling up while the walls that she had built for protection were slowly, oh so slowly, coming down.

Bradley looked at the ROI calculation he'd been fiddling with for the past two hours, but for once the numbers held no interest to him. Sophia had been there for lunch at one o'clock, leaving at two fifteen on the dot, but it wasn't enough.

Saving his document, he headed down the stairs out to the front porch, where he was pretty sure he'd find her with Missy. It was a Thursday, which meant their usual activity for the day was pushed later because the blond would go into town and help at the veterinary clinic.

Although Bart was more than happy to just have Missy live on the ranch without ever having to work, she still muckraked in the barns about twice a week and worked in town on Tuesdays and Thursdays. Everyone knew she was saving up for her own animal rescue, but what she didn't know was that Bart had been setting funds aside for exactly that as a wedding present. He hoped Missy wore waterproof mascara to her ceremony, because she was going to bawl like a baby.

...would Sophia want to work on something other than her commissions eventually? Was there going to *be* an eventually? He'd set up her insurance, and she'd scheduled counseling out four weeks ahead so he knew that she would be around for at least that, but when he tried to think of the longer term, like a year, or a few years, he couldn't. The picture was hazy, full of too many what-ifs and unknown variables.

But at the same time, he couldn't *not* picture her there.

It was like a Mobius sort of fantasy. Both there and not there. He didn't like the uncertainty of that, so he sat down on the porch swing while he watched Missy try to lead Sophia through a simple waltz.

He didn't really understand the rhyme or reason behind Missy's lessons, but Sophia still seemed to love them nonetheless. Sure, at first it had all been things that were useful for her to know, things to make her feel comforted and protected. The self-defense, the grappling, how to disarm an opponent. He had never been aware that Missy had so much knowledge about fighting, but when he asked Bart, the muscled man had gotten all dreamy eyed and said something about his beautiful Amazon, so Bradley had kind of glazed over.

But once all of the practical stuff was out of the way, there'd been painting, and learning how to do a cartwheel, simple repair sewing, how to shoe a horse, mixing the perfect water-to-soap ratio for really good bubbles, how to catch a fish, how to clean a fish, makeup, it was such a wide range of things that he could never really guess what was next.

Then again, maybe it was all stuff that people would normally learn if they were given the chance to have a real life. Sophia had basically been snatched up and groomed since she was seventeen. Not allowed to be her own person. Not allowed to do her own things. Explore what she liked and disliked. No, that time had been robbed from her.

So maybe... maybe the whole point of Missy's activities was to give Sophia all of that time back.

Bradley whistled to himself. Bart was right. Missy *was* real good at understanding what people needed. Pulling out his phone, he put in a reminder to himself to get her a very nice gift card for one of those pet sites online that Bart said she approved of.

After that was done, he contented himself to watching until they finished, making sure to stand up and clap when they were done.

"Thank you, thank you," Missy said with an exaggerated bow. "I live to serve."

But Sophia had a different reaction. "Don't tease me," she said, coming up onto the porch and pushing playfully at his arm. "I wasn't *that* bad."

"I never said you were," Bradley retorted. "I was admiring your efforts. ...and the durability of Missy's shoes."

"Steel-toed boots!" Missy called as she walked off in the direction of her and Bart's cabin.

As for Sophia, she just cracked up laughing.

Strangely enough, Bradley loved the sound. It was so unchecked, unflinching. Although Sophia was healing, she was never very loud. Always keeping her voice down as if she was afraid she might trigger something terrible if she dared go above a certain level. He supposed it was possible that she had subconsciously trained herself to be quiet as a survival tactic, but that made him cherish the moments where she was loud all the more.

"Yeah, I really am not good at keeping a count. And I thought all Latinas were supposed to have rhythm."

"I'm sure you have rhythm. It's just *your* rhythm."

"Are you trying to find a nice way to tell me that I march to the beat of my own drum?"

"Wait, is that not a nice saying itself? Because people have been telling me that since I was three."

"Well yeah, but that's because you're real weird."

Bradley huffed in faux affront. "Excuse you, I'm rich. It's called *eccentric*."

"Yeah, well why don't you eccentric me up a glass of lemonade then? I'm parched."

"That's not how you use that word. It's an adjective, not a verb."

She placed a hand on his chest as she moved around him to the front door. "Anything is a verb if you try hard enough. So, did you just come down for the show or is there a sudden accounting apocalypse I should know about?"

For a moment Bradley had forgotten his purpose for even leaving his office. But that was what being with Sophia was like. The rest of the world fell away, and it was just them. "I, uh, I was actually thinking that it's been a while since we left the house. If we wanna keep the ruse up, I thought we should go into town for a date."

"Right. Only for the ruse, of course."

"Yeah, of course," he agreed quickly.

"I don't know. I don't really have anything else to wear for something like that fancy restaurant we went to before."

"Actually, I was thinking something different."

She lifted one of her eyebrows. "Hmmm?"

"I might have overheard you telling one of the girls that you've never seen a musical outside of a high school production. There's a pretty good theater in the city, and they have a great one running. That is… if you'd want to go."

Her hand left the door, and she turned around fully to look at him. "You want to take me to a play?"

"Well, a musical, but yeah."

"I… I don't have anything nice to wear. Unless you think I could use that blue dress again?"

"No, it'll be a bit too cold, I think. How about we go into the city and find you something? We could even go to a salon for your hair and makeup if you want. Make a whole afternoon and evening of it?"

She stared at him like he had grown another head. "You want to... take me shopping for a dress, then to an expensive salon to get done up, then to a theater?"

"And maybe some ice cream later? You know, if it's not too cold."

"But..." She looked troubled, and he wondered if he had gone overboard. If he had made her uncomfortable. "...but that's so much."

"Is it?"

She nodded. "*Why?*"

"Why what?"

"Why would you wanna do that?"

He raised his eyebrows, his go-to expression. "I just want to. I think it would be fun."

"I..." After hesitating, she seemed to come to a decision and nodded. "Okay. Yeah. It does sound fun."

"Really?" Relief flooded through him and he stood up straighter. He had come up with the whole outfit thing on the fly, so he hadn't exactly planned it properly. He needed to iron out some details and buy the tickets. Thankfully it was a Thursday in the middle of the run, so he didn't think they'd be sold out. "Okay. That's good. Right."

"Do I have time to shower and get changed?"

"Yeah, yeah of course. Do whatever you need. I'll go make sure everything's ready once you're out."

"Okay, sounds like a plan."

He *wished* he had a plan. Like so many things with Sophia, he rarely thought outside of the now.

She headed inside, and he busied himself with some very quick online ordering. Because if he was going to take Sophia out on a night on the town, he was going to make sure it was the best night he could give her.

"It's not too late to back down now."

Bradley looked over his arm to Sophia, who was curled up in his passenger's seat as usual. She had on comfortable sweatpants and a light T-shirt, her thick hair still slightly damp from her shower, and Bradley wondered if she'd ever looked more beautiful. Something about seeing her there all relaxed and in her natural state, smiling softly and resting easy, looked so perfect to him.

"Why, you having second thoughts?"

"No. Just giving you a way out in case you didn't think this through."

He shrugged. "I'm taking a beautiful woman out on a fun date. What's there to think through?"

"You're taking your *fake* fiancé on a *fake* date but spending a whole lot of real money."

He shrugged. "Money is meant to be spent. People and memories are what's priceless."

"Hah, spoken like a rich man."

"What, you don't agree?"

"Only partially. I know that people and memories are what make life worth living. But if you're sick with pneumonia and don't have health insurance, money sure does mean a whole lot. Or if you're about to get evicted. Or if your kid desperately needs braces, but you can't afford it. Or if you're hungry with an empty cupboard and wallet. In all those cases, money could be considered priceless too."

"Alright, you have a point."

"I do try." She looked expectantly to the door, and Bradley smiled, going around to open it for her. "You're not just doing this so you have an excuse to not see a musical by yourself, are you?" she asked as he opened it and held out his hand.

"You caught me. That was my master plan all along. As if I couldn't drag Ma to these any time I wanted."

"Please, this would be way past her bedtime." She landed on the ground but kept a hold of his hand. He stayed still a moment, just in case she changed her mind, but when that moment passed, he took it in stride.

"So, where are we going first?"

"Chastity told me that this stretch had some of the better clothing boutiques in the city, so I figured we could walk along, look in the windows and go in if we see anything that you like."

"Huh, it's really that easy?"

"Well, only if they have something you like."

"And if they don't?"

"Well, sweats and T-shirts aren't the normal play uniform, but it's not like they'll kick us out. Or... I don't think they will."

"Right, so find a dress."

"Or a nice shirt and pants."

"Please, we have a way better chance of finding a dress that fits than pants that are the right length for my short legs."

"I think your legs are just fine."

She laughed and kicked one of them upwards. "Why, you been lookin' at them?"

"I confess to nothing. I am the perfect gentleman."

"Uh-huh. Keep telling yourself that."

They devolved into friendly banter as they exited the parking garage and headed out onto the street. But the moment they passed the first boutique window, Sophia fell silent, stopping in her tracks to stare at the beautifully decorated window.

Bradley smiled, enjoying the look of wonder on her face. He didn't say anything, just letting the moment go on as long as she needed, but a flicker of concern rose in him when tears started to well up in her eyes.

"Hey, are you okay?"

She nodded, gulping down some air and hastily rubbing at her eyes. "Yeah. I'm fine. I just... I remember when I was a little girl, it was summer, and my mother and I were shopping in St. Louis. We were on the upper side for some reason, I can't recall, but we walked past a storefront just like this.

"I thought it was the most beautiful thing that I had ever seen. I wanted to go in so desperately, but I remember her telling me that those places weren't for us. I didn't understand what she meant, but it always stuck with me. That nice things weren't for me, and nice places where rich white people with great vocabularies and college degrees were someplace I'd never belong."

"Sophia..."

She turned to him and flashed him such a brilliant smile that his comforting words stilled on his tongue. "Yet here I am. I have my choice to go into any of these. Or *all* of them, if I wanted. Because I deserve nice things. I belong in nice places. And I'm finally beginning to believe that."

A bubbling, sweeping sort of warmth rushed through Bradley at that, like the floodgates that had been holding so much back were finally open. Despite practically living in the same house for almost a quarter of a year, he didn't think he'd ever heard Sophia say anything nice about herself. Or that she deserved something. To have her say those words entirely on her own told him that they really were doing right by her. That they were helping. And that was all he wanted.

Well, and maybe he also wanted to hold her like he had that night in his truck, but that was inappropriate, and he was actively trying *not* to do that.

"I'm glad you are," he managed to say with a somewhat steady voice. "Because you do deserve nice things. You really do."

"Thanks. That means a lot."

Their eyes locked onto each others, and he felt more connected to her than he ever had to someone who wasn't family. But the longer they stared, the more intense the moment grew, until it was too much. Too heavy for what they were supposed to be doing right now, which was shopping.

Clearing his throat, Bradley tore his gaze away. "So, you want to go into this one?"

"I... I think we should walk the entire boulevard and look at all of them, then on our way back decide which to go into."

"Sure. Whatever you want."

"Funny thing, I think I'm finally able to actually want things."

"I guess I've got some good timing then."

17

———

Sophia

*I*f four months earlier someone had told her that she would be walking down some high-end boulevard with her pick of any store to go into and any of the clothes that were inside, she would have told them they were crazy.

And yet, that was exactly how she was spending her afternoon and early evening, leisurely strolling hand-in-hand with Bradley.

She felt... well, she didn't really have a word for it, but it was the most amazing feeling. It was a mix of safe, and happy, and excited, and all sorts of good, fuzzy things that made her toes curl.

Did Bradley know? Did he really understand what he did for her? She had spent all of the past two years looking over her shoulder, always feeling her ex watching her, always fearing he was right there, waiting for her. But when she was with him, she didn't feel that same unending terror. She felt safe. Although her ex's father had tried to use his connections, it was clear that *he* was afraid of Bradley. Not since that fight in the inn had he faced Bradley, and she knew he wouldn't.

Because her ex was a coward. She knew that now. He had always been stronger than her, and she thought smarter than her, but the truth was that he was weak, and the only way he thought he could keep her was if he cut her down until she was weak like him too.

She was still angry that she had lost so much of her life to him. That his tendrils still had a home in her brain, whispering to trust no one. Whispering that she could never do anything right. Making her feel like she was a slut for wearing make-up or for wearing a pretty outfit. But she was stopping that.

Sure, it wasn't going to be easy. It wasn't going to be quick. Her first meeting with her therapist hadn't touched on a single one of the issues she knew that she needed to work on. That first visit had been about explaining her situation and outlining her goals for treatment.

It would be easy if Sophia could take her whole brain out and give it a good scrub, but that wasn't how life worked.

But in the meantime, she would enjoy everything Bradley was willing to give her.

Which, at the moment, certainly seemed like quite a lot.

"Let's try this one," she said, pointing to a storefront as they circled back around.

There were some loose and beaded dresses in the window complete with practical looking shoes on display. Although Sophia loved the dress that Missy had ordered her, she was still a bit uncomfortable in anything too formfitting. She remembered once wearing something similar for a date night with her ex, and he'd flown into a rage, accusing her of trying to seduce everyone around her and being a slut.

But Bradley would never do that. She knew that. She had been tricked by her ex's Prince Charming act when she was young and naïve, but that wasn't what was happening with the Miller son. He wasn't anything like her ex.

Which also meant that most of the time, she had no idea how she was supposed to act around him, but he didn't seem to mind.

"Alright, you look around for something you like, and I'll uh, stand in the corner and try not to get my dirty hands on anything."

Sophia gave Bradley a look. "Huh-uh. Don't you act like you've been out in the fields all day. I don't think I've even seen so much as grit under your nails. You wanted to shop, then let's shop."

He huffed for only a moment before giving in. Sophia smiled to herself and led him over to what looked to be the right area for dresses in her size. She got the feeling that she could ask almost anything from the man, and he would give it to her, which confused her a bit. He didn't seem interested in kissing her again, or really pursuing her romantically, but he doted on her and cared about pleasing her and sometimes when he looked at her...

Ah, it wasn't the right time for those kinds of thoughts.

"What's your favorite color?" she asked, looking over the dresses. She'd done some research while she was waiting for the shower water to warm up back at the house, and figured she wanted something stately but not over the top. It was a nice evening, not a gala.

Oh goodness, would Bradley ever take her to a gala? Did she *want* to go to a gala? It wasn't exactly ever an option before, and he didn't really seem like the gala type, but she was sure if she even hinted at it that he would whisk her away when the opportunity presented itself.

That thought made her dizzy.

"Uh, I don't really have one."

"Nonsense. Everyone has a favorite color."

"I don't."

Something about his tone caught her attention, and she looked him over. His feet were wider apart, and his arms were crossed. He was looking past her shoulder, not making eye contact with her. If there was one thing that Bradley was all about, it was that long, persistent gaze whenever he was figuring something out.

"You're lying."

He shifted a bit. "It's... it's just dumb."

"How can a favorite color be dumb."

He shrugged. "You wouldn't believe me if I told you."

Now Sophia was officially intrigued. "Come on, it's just a color! Why are you treating it like your secret weakness or something? What, is it the color of some competitor's brand and you don't want your family to know?"

"No, nothing like that. It's just," he sighed, then rolled his eyes, but eventually gave in like she knew he would. "It uh, it's... it's pink."

"Pink?" she repeated. She hadn't been sure what to expect, but that wasn't it.

"Yeah. It's been that way ever since we were little. To me, it just seemed like a lot of great things are pink."

"Oh, really?"

"Yeah, like the little footpads on kittens, the noses of some of our cows. Little piglets. I remember when Ma was just beginning to go grey, she dyed her hair red. It was pretty, but then it faded to this rosy color and I thought it was just the most magical thing."

His tone grew a bit wistful, and Sophia watched the myriad of emotions cross his face.

"Pink is the color of the sky right where it switches from twilight to daylight. I always liked that time, and I'd wake up early to read a book and watch the sunrise. Pink is the color of new skin and healing. The color of blush on a beautiful woman after you compliment her." His eyes flicked to her face. "The color of soft lips before you kiss them all red."

That made her heartrate rocket up, and it almost seemed like he leaned towards her, but he recovered quickly. "Heck, it goes great with just about everything and ranges all the way from the duskiest, faintest flush all the way up to neon. I made the mistake of telling my brothers once, and, well... they wouldn't let me live it down. Nowadays I just say red but... I don't know, it didn't seem right to lie about it to you."

"Pink is a great color," Sophia said, feeling special that he had trusted her with something he was obviously sensitive about. Sure, maybe it was just a color, but it meant a lot. "I'm sure I can find something."

"Aw, you don't have to base your dress on what I—"

"Oh, look! There's one here!"

She grabbed the garment and pulled it out, pleased to see it was around her size. Looking around, she spotted the dressing room and pulled him towards it.

"Wait here," she said, pointing him to a spot just outside of it.

He did, and she headed inside. It was a quick matter to get out of her casual clothes, but when she went to try the dress on, she was disappointed to find that it was swimming on her. And not in the comforting, protective way she liked. Just more like a bag.

Well, that sucked.

"Looks like this isn't the one," she said, getting dressed. "But that's alright. There was another shop I wanted to go to."

"You really don't have to get a pink dress just because I like the color. I like a lot of colors."

"It's too late. My mind's made up. You just keep track of the time to make sure I don't run out."

"Yes, ma'am."

Hanging the dress up on the hook at the door, she grabbed Bradley's hand and headed out of the store. She couldn't remember the last time that she'd had so much fun, and the night was just getting started.

THIS WAS IT.

Sophia looked in the mirror, turning this way and that. They were in their third shop, and even though she loved spending time with Bradley, she was starting to be a little over the whole shopping thing.

But all of it was worth it, because she was standing in a dressing room, dressed like a princess.

The dress was a beautiful, light pink, reminding her of pink baby's breath and shimmering magic. It was fitted at the top, with lace sleeves, but the bottom was loose and flowing in multiple layers of chiffon. Or some other lightweight, translucent fabric. Sophia wasn't exactly an expert.

"I think I found it!" she said excitedly, knowing that Bradley was right out there where she had left him.

"Really?"

It pleased her that he sounded almost as excited as she felt. "Yeah, really."

"Well then, come on out! Let me see!"

Sophia took a deep breath and then opened the door of the small changing room, giving a little twirl. It wasn't like her to be showy, but she thought it was definitely a special occasion.

"So, what do you think?"

But he just stood there, staring at her.

"Uh, do you not like it?"

"Uh, uh no, I love it. You... you look beautiful." He huffed again. "I mean, beautiful doesn't even cut it. You almost don't even look real. Like someone just plucked you out of a book and put you here."

She felt that bubbling warmth rush through her again. Just like it did whenever he landed one of those compliments on her. She'd never met anyone who could dole out nice things so matter-of-factly.

"Really? What kind of book?"

"I dunno. Maybe a fantasy with elves and princesses and magic. Or maybe some historical romance with castles and royalty, maybe a little intrigue thrown in."

"Wow, that good, huh?" She took a step towards him, looking up at him through her lashes. He was so tall, compared to her, and he was the shortest of all his brothers. The Millers were some giant people, alright, with even diminutive Ma being only an inch or so taller than her.

He stiffened slightly, just like he always did when they were close. Did she disgust him? Did he hate it?

"More than that," he said. "I've just never been very good with words."

"I dunno, you seem to do just fine to me." She took another step.

"Well, that's good to know."

A final step. They were almost chest to chest, and her neck was craned upwards to look at his handsome face. "Is it?"

"Is it what?"

"Good to know."

"Uh, yeah. Yeah, it is."

She didn't have a plan, didn't think. Instead, she just pushed herself up on her tiptoes and...

"That dress really is a lovely color on you! Now we just need to get you some shoes to go with it!"

The voice of the salesperson brought them both back into the moment, and Bradley stepped away. "Uh, shoes. Yeah, you're right. Sophia, what's your size?"

"Between six and seven and a half depending on the brand," she answered, somewhat in a daze from the sudden mood whiplash.

"Really? Geez, not even shoes are simple for women, huh?"

"Blame the fashion industry and the misogynistic demands it caters to."

His eyes narrowed at that. "You been talking to Dani?"

"No, why?"

"Nothing, just sounds like something she said in the middle of her five-minute rant about purses."

"I hate purses," Sophia said quickly. "They're why women's clothes never have good pockets."

"And *there* it is." He shook his head, chuckling as he followed the sales associate. "You really do fit in just right."

Sophia walked after him, acting like everything was perfectly normal, but inside his words made her glow.

She fit in.

She *belonged.*

And for the moment, that was all she needed.

18

———

Bradley

Bradley felt like he was ten feet tall as he entered the theater, Sophia all dolled up and on his arm with her ring shining on her finger.

Yeah, he knew their engagement was fake. And yeah, he knew that one day she might leave him when they got her whole ex thing fully settled. But none of that mattered. All that mattered was that she was there, with him, sharing an experience.

"Oh, my *goodness!*" she whispered next to him, her head swiveling this way and that as she looked around.

After buying her that perfect, perfect dress that fit her exactly how a beautiful gown should, they'd gone to get some crepes from one of the local shops then headed off to a salon. It was strange, Bradley had never been much of one for shopping or even spending his own money, but he loved everything about his little trip with Sophia.

Seeing her laugh, seeing her smile, seeing her brows furrow as she held up a dress and inspected it, how excited she got when she found one in her size. And when she had first come out of the dressing room in what she was wearing now? Priceless. Utterly priceless.

Thankfully, the salon process had been pretty fast. Sophia had asked for long layers—not that he knew what that meant—but she seemed pleased with what the salon had done. They cut off a few inches and put something in it that apparently gave it 'texture and body.' Bradley didn't understand even half the science of it, but he did appreciate how it accentuated Sophia's beautiful bone structure.

Her eyelashes had what looked like gold shimmer and somehow they were magically twice as long, but perhaps what caught his attention most of all were her dusky pink lips.

It was hard for his eyes not to keep sliding there, memories replaying in his head the instant they did. He wondered what it would feel like to press his lips to hers again, to show her all that he felt, all that he had been holding back.

But he couldn't, so instead, he tried his best not to look.

"I can't believe I'm really here." Sophia breathed out a sigh. "When I was younger, I always wanted to see plays on Broadway, but of course that wasn't something that we could ever afford."

"Well, this isn't quite Broadway, but it's pretty nice."

"I'll say!" She pulled him towards the stairs, which were lined with a lush green rug with gold embellishments. "Are we this way?"

"We are, but there's an elevator if you want to take it."

"No, I want to see all of this place. We can take the elevator down when it's time to go home and my feet are aching from these heels."

"You know we're going to be sitting down, right?"

"Yeah, but that still puts pressure on my feet," she said it like it was silly to think otherwise. "And crossing your legs is terrible for your hips, and I am *not* gonna end up with a hip replacement at fifty-five like my *abuelita*."

"Wait, sitting cross-legged will mess up your hips?"

She only barely paid attention to Bradley as she strode up the stairs, pausing half-way up to stare at one of the chandeliers above. It wasn't the most ostentatious one he'd ever seen, but it was still pretty showy.

"Yup and sitting on your wallet can mess up your back. Makes your sacrum tilted."

"Wait, my what now?"

"Your sacrum. You know, the bony thing that makes up your pelvic wall. It's like, a big deal for all the rotating our hips do. Stabilizes stuff, has a lot of muscles attached to it?"

"How do you even *know* that?"

"Uh, drawing, I guess. Helps to know a lot of anatomy. You're not the only one who likes to read, you know."

"I see."

Bradley had never thought that Sophia was dumb, not even close, but it was interesting to hear her spout off something a bit nerdy so casually.

...he was pretty sure he liked it.

They reached the top of the stairs, and she took his hand again. "Okay, now, where do we sit?"

"This way."

Smiling, he led her to the side. He hadn't been able to get a seat in the sweet spot he usually liked, but there had been a box seat open. He figured that would definitely be an experience for Sophia, so he paid the extra amount happily.

"I think you're gonna like this," he said, heading towards where he was pretty sure it was. He wasn't usually one for the box seats, preferring to be closer to the stage, but Ma sometimes got a little overcrowded during intermission and final exits, so he would get the more closed off area whenever she came with him.

"Oh man, this is awesome!" she said once he gave their tickets to the attendant at the hall leading to the box seats. "I feel so fancy."

"Glad that you're enjoying yourself," he said, settling into their comfier seats. "I really hope you enjoy this."

She gave him a happy smile. "I can't imagine I won't."

"Oh. My. Goodness gracious on a cracker!" Sophia said, clapping her hands together as they got into the truck. "That. Was. Amazing!"

Bradley grinned to himself, feeling quite accomplished. "I'm glad you liked it."

"Liked it!" she cried, clapping some more. "That was, well, that was possibly the coolest thing I've ever seen! That big number where all of the extras came out and they were singing that one mean part of the song, and then the other part was all hopeful and looking towards the future, and then there was the part where the wife found out he was cheating on her. Oh man! And the *affair!* It didn't want it to happen, but at the same time, how could it *not* happen. I was like, powerless as I watched, but

I didn't want to look away. I just... I can't believe that I've never seen a real production before!"

Bradley glanced over to her as much as he could, considering he was starting to drive through the city and back home. "So, you wouldn't mind going to another one of those with me? They usually have several different shows per year, sometimes with some special holiday events."

"Would I?"

She flailed a bit, and if that wasn't just the most adorable thing that he had ever seen in his entire life.

"Yeah. Please! And you don't have to go and buy me a dress every time."

"Aw, well that's a shame then, because I certainly liked buying a dress for you."

"Even though I dragged you into four different stores."

He shrugged, more of a habit at this point than anything else. "Variety is the spice of life."

She reached over and rested her hand on top of where his was resting on the stick shift. "You're too good to me, you know that?"

Like every time she touched him, Bradley was suddenly acutely aware of everything about her. The soft puffs of her breath, the gentle waft of her perfume, how soft the skin of her fingers felt atop his rougher hand, her nails only lightly grazing him.

"I would definitely disagree on that. I feel like I haven't done nearly enough."

"Well, you're wrong."

"Oh, so that's how it is now?"

"That's how it is." She tilted her head back and let out a

long, loud laugh. It was boundless and fearless and perfect in every way, and soon Bradley joined in.

He wished he could bottle the feeling she filled him with, because everyone deserved to feel that great. Well, everyone except for her ex and all of his family. They could all go jump in the lake if anyone asked him.

Eventually, however, their mirth settled and the conversation lulled. Although that normally meant it was time to sit in the quiet, Sophia started humming one of the songs from the musical. The more she went on, the louder she grew, until it was clear to hear the melody over the hum of his engine.

"I didn't know you can sing."

"Huh? Oh, I can't sing."

"Sounds like you're carrying a tune fine enough to me."

"Humming is not the same as singing."

"No, but they are related. You should sing for me."

"What?" She barked out another laugh, this one sharper and dryer. "Never in a million years."

He fake pouted. "Fine, if not for me, then how about for the entire cast?"

One of her thick eyebrows raised. "What do you mean?"

"I mean," reaching behind the seat, he felt around for the caddy he kept back in the extended cab. When he felt it, he hauled it over and placed a full CD caddy into her lap. "I have the entire soundtrack, both with the original cast and the touring one."

"Wow, you really *do* love musicals," she said.

"Why wouldn't I? I was in drama club, you know."

"Ha, it's because you're totally a nerd."

"Oh, am I now?"

"Yeah." She grinned at him as she found the CD and brandished it with a flourish. "But it's okay. I like it."

"Is that so?"

"Uh-huh."

"Alright. Well that's good to know."

"Is it?"

He recognized it as a callback to their conversation earlier. Something about that pleased him, like they had a special link together. An inside joke. "Yeah. It's very good to know."

She seemed to like his answer, and her grin grew wider. Taking the CD from her, he slid it in. Soon, the music filled his cab, and she did start singing along. Sure, she wasn't the next prima donna, but she was just as good if not better than Bradley was back in his heyday.

They spent the rest of the hour ride singing and enjoying themselves, not a care in the world. Their own little bubble that no one else could touch.

But that was the thing about bubbles; they always had to burst, and eventually, they were pulling right back into the garage.

"Well, I guess this is good night," he said, wishing that it absolutely wasn't.

But Sophia looked at him demurely. "I dunno. Nobody's opened my door for me yet."

"Ah, you're right. How could I forget?" Turning off the truck, he slid out and crossed over to her side.

"Thank you, Bradley," Sophia murmured as she got out of the truck.

Her body brushed against when she got out. But Bradley hadn't been anticipating that, and the movement brought them right up against each other, her soft form barely brushing against his.

Once more he froze, shocked by the sudden deluge of details all about her. It would be so easy to tilt his head down and kiss her, to have their mouths move together like they had in his truck, to taste her, memorize every detail of her.

But the only reason they had kissed at all was because she was terrified that he was going to kick her out. He couldn't use that fear to take advantage of her. And as much as he wanted to kiss her and never stop, he wanted her safety, health, and happiness even more.

Pulling away, he walked over to the door leading to the house and opened it for her. But as she walked past, he knew that he was going to dream of her for the rest of the week.

Oh boy, he was in such a mess. But perhaps the craziest thing was that not a single ounce of himself wanted to get out of it.

19
___

Sophia

"**W**hat do you mean you don't have a dressed picked out yet?"

"Or an idea of wedding colors?"

"Don't you at least have a *season* to shoot for?"

Sophia stared with wide eyes at Dani, Missy, and Keiko. Finally, after a solid month since the diner incident and two more meetings with her new therapist, she felt comfortable enough to go back into town. So, the girls had decided to all have a nice lunch at the diner and make another try at her idea of making dinner for the whole family.

Unfortunately, Chastity couldn't make it. She was up in the Big Apple doing some sort of internet award show thing and wouldn't be back until Saturday morning. But even without the oldest and most experienced of the group, they were still having a good time.

Or at least, Sophia was until someone asked if she was going to have any bridesmaids. When Sophia replied that she hadn't given the wedding any thought yet, the shocked ladies in the group had a million questions.

Sophia tried to explain. "Like I said, it's not really on my mind given everything going on."

"But don't you have even an idea?" Dani furrowed her brow as if to think. "Look, I'm not much of one for fancy shindigs either, but here's something you could try. I didn't want all that hanging over my head for a year, so I did everything as fast as I could and handed off the rest to Benji. *He* really loved a lot of that whole stuff. Have you checked in with Bradley? Maybe wedding planning would be something he'd enjoy doing?"

No. She hadn't checked with Bradley. Because they were never going to *get* married. The thought crept bitterly along the back of her tongue, and for once she wished that he hadn't come up with the whole ruse. She felt like they were stuck in this weird place—pretending to be what they weren't and never being able to grow into something more because their foundation was all lies. Maybe... maybe if they weren't fake engaged, if they had just told Ma right off the bat that it was fake, there would be a chance for something to happen between them.

But then again, that was only a maybe. Even if they didn't have the fake engagement, even if there wasn't a shiny ring on her finger, there was no guarantee that Bradley would ever go for someone like her.

Yeah, she was making an effort. And yeah, she was healing, but she was still just so... *damaged.* And she hated it. She hated that her ex still had such an influence on her even when she hadn't seen him since the grocery store. She hated that she sometimes woke up in a cold sweat in the middle of the night, sure that he was right by her bed, ready to drag her away from the peace that she had found.

"We haven't talked about it much. Maybe if we can go three months without my ex popping up again, we'll have time to care about things like DJs and colors and dresses."

Dani nodded like that made all the sense in the world. "Sounds like a plan to me. Practical, I like it."

"I'm not sure," Keiko said softly, calmly cutting her burger up with a knife and fork. Because of course she would. Although her new friend wasn't prissy or stuck up, Sophia had learned that she was very particular about messes, food, and getting wet. "It sounds like avoidance to me."

"Big words from someone who can't eat a burger without a napkin tucked into their neck and on their lap."

The corner of her lip turned up at that. "I think you, of all people, know that we cope with our mental illnesses in different ways."

"Wait, mental illness, what?"

"Keiko, you don't have to—" Dani started.

But the slender woman just raised her hand. "I have OCD. Mild, but when I was younger, I fell into an eating disorder. It allowed me to have some control because my illness left me feeling powerless and overwhelmed."

Sophia just stared at Keiko, astounded. Perfect, poised Keiko was screwy in the head like her?

Keiko continued, "Long story short, it's been a pretty fraught journey to get where I am now, with a whole lot of work and mishaps, but I have my coping mechanisms. And one of them is making sure food touches nowhere but the inside of my mouth. My therapist and I worked out a whole list of strategies and backup plans for if I relapse or have an especially bad flare-up."

"Wait, you see a *therapist?*"

"Of course. My parents do too. I am incredibly fortunate that they've always had great insurance."

Sophia couldn't believe it. Keiko was always so put together —and charming. And she was so *smart*. It made her feel so much less broken, gave her so much hope. Maybe... if she really applied herself, she could be the kind of woman that Bradley would go for. The kind who fit in at fancy musicals or galas and his high-class world.

Wouldn't that be something?

"Why are you smiling?" Keiko asked, looking like she might have an idea of exactly why.

"Nothing. Just appreciating your perspective. Almost makes me brave enough to actually think about the future."

"Well, thank you. That's certainly a compliment." She finished cutting a piece of her burger, lifted it to her mouth, and thoughtfully chewed it before swallowing. Her actions were very deliberate, but no one talked. Keiko had just that sort of weight to her words. "But even with that said, it's still avoidance."

Sophia groaned. "Come on, we're not on that again, are we?"

"We never left it, actually," Keiko said *almost* smugly. "You only tried to steer the conversation elsewhere. Tried, but didn't succeed."

"Right, well I'm gonna keep right on with that avoidance until we talk about something else."

"What about a compromise here, ladies?" Missy asked,

leaning forward. "We won't talk about the wedding, but what about some peripherals? Have you thought about a dress for your rehearsal dinner? The reception? Clothes for your honeymoon? Maybe a bathing suit or two? Or what about," she lowered her voice and wiggled her eyebrows. "Maybe something for your wedding night?"

Sophia felt herself flush brightly. Sure, she was really attracted to Bradley, and sure, she had been ready to throw her body at him, but once he made it clear that that would *never* be a condition of her stay, she realized that she wasn't ready for anything like that.

Missy had the gall to look a bit sheepish. "Sorry, was that too far? I know you and Bradley are private."

Yeah, that was one way to put it.

"It's okay. It's just easier if I don't think about it."

Dani let out a quiet laugh, nearly done devouring her buffalo chicken fingers. "Girl, tell me about it. Sometimes I feel like I've got to carry a bottle of ice water around when I'm alone with Benji. It's easy to get carried away."

She wished that Bradley had an issue with getting carried away. No, he was composed and in control all the time. Much better than her. Sometimes, when they were especially close to each other, it took all of her control not to throw her arms around him and kiss him like she had in the truck.

She'd been desperate and maybe a little drugged at the time, so the memory was blurry in her head. She wished that she had been clear-headed, so she could go over every detail of it, but if she was clear-headed, it probably never would have happened.

But still, she could recall the feel of the stubble on his face, rasping against her chin. How strong and big his hands were as they held her firmly, binding her to him. She could feel the power in his broad fingers, and yet she knew he would never use them to hurt her. And that thought was uncanny. The closeness had been like a warm, soothing liquid poured right into her soul, and it'd been so easy to slip into the heat of it all.

"Whoa, you're bright red there. You okay?"

"I'm fine," she answered quickly before grabbing her water and quickly chugging it down.

"Oh, I have an idea," Missy said, clapping her hands. "How about this weekend we all go to the mall and do a little shopping for the peripherals? You know, ease your toes into the water so maybe thinking about the wedding isn't quite so scary. I'll text Chastity so she'll be there too, and it'll be like the girl squad is back together! We haven't done that since before..."

"Before the grocery," Sophia finished for her.

"Yeah. Since before that."

Sophia debated a moment, thinking hard. They didn't understand why she was so reticent to talk about the future with Bradley because they didn't understand there was no future. They meant well, but shopping around for things that would never happen might be a trigger for the dark thoughts and feelings inside of her.

But then again, pretending had gotten her this far. Maybe it wouldn't be so bad. And maybe... maybe if she got a few things, she could treasure them for whenever things inevitably went south and she and Bradley had to begin their fake breakup.

Except that breakup wasn't going to feel fake at all. Because her feelings were very real.

"I THINK... I think that would be fun."

"Alright!" Missy held up her hand, and Dani rolled her eyes before high fiving it.

"You know, I did have plans, but I guess I can cancel them."

Keiko chuckled, setting her knife and fork down. "Your only plan was watching your brothers like a hawk while they work around your ranch. I'm sure they'll be glad to be free for a single afternoon."

Dani let out an exasperated sigh. "Keiko, you don't *always* have to know everything all the time. Besides, my brothers are still healing. You can't blame me for being protective."

"No, but I could blame you for being *over*protective," Keiko said.

"Hey, let's go back to Sophia's thing. That was much more fun than this," Dani said.

Sophia shook her head firmly. "Nah, I'm good. I'd much rather the Keiko-scope be on you."

"Ladies, ladies, I'll take the hit." Missy leaned forward so she was almost across the table with her long, muscled frame. Reaching out, she laid a hand over Keiko's and smiled with those perfect red lips of her. "Honey, has anyone ever told you that you like to point out the issues of others around you because it gives you comfort that you aren't the only person with demons to wrestle?"

Keiko sputtered a moment, actually looking caught off guard, then laughed.

Dani howled. "My Lord! Keiko just got Keiko'd, I never thought I'd see the day!"

The group all laughed, and Sophia realized how good it was to share struggles with other women who could help put them in perspective. Soon the conversation shifted to the new pet store in the mall and how much Missy hated puppy mills. It was a much easier topic for everyone, listening to her proselytize about something she was passionate about, and Sophia sat back.

Shopping on the weekend. She could do that. Maybe if she talked to Bradley about it beforehand, he'd get the idea in his head that maybe, just maybe, there could be a real future to them. As real as the things that she purchased.

Yeah, like that would ever happen. She couldn't help but scoff to herself.

But still, it was nice to dream. Even if it was impossible.

20

<hr>

Sophia

"Okay, you have an olive tint to your skin, so purple, certain shades of pink, maroon, burgundy, and burnt oranges will look great on you," Chasity said as they walked into the large doors of the mall. "But honestly, almost all colors will look good on you except for some pastels and anything green."

"Why no green?" Dani asked, looking around with a bored expression.

Sophia knew that fashion wasn't *really* Dani's deal unless it was socks. The woman had a weird obsession with colorful and silly socks, ranging from multicolor neons to ones covered with cartoon characters.

"It brings out the green in your skin tone. Not really what we want to emphasize."

Missy whistled. "Man, this stuff is such a science. I don't know how you remember all of it."

Chastity shrugged. "I don't know. I've been interested in it way back in the day, ever since the costuming from drama club."

"Wait," Sophia said, eyes going wide. "You were in drama club? Did you do any shows with Bradley?" How did she not know that? If Chastity was involved with acting, maybe she would have insider knowledge about that part of Bradley's life.

"Oh no, he was a freshman after I graduated. My era was with the eldest three Miller brothers."

"Actually, I was the one who was in drama club with Bradley," Keiko said, carefully sipping coffee through a long straw. "I think he was the one who figured out my unorthodox eating schedule and tattled on me. He was the only one who liked reading as much as I did, so we spent a lot of time together."

Sophia certainly hadn't expected it, but a spike of jealousy lanced through her. That was incredibly silly of her. "Oh, did uh, something happen between you two?"

Keiko took a long sip of her coffee. "Why do you ask?"

"Aw, come off it," Dani said, nudging her. "This is a shopping spree, not the time for you to analyze all our innermost secrets."

Keiko chuckled lightly. "Fine. If you're asking if we dated or anything, I was completely uninterested in anyone at the time. All that mattered to me were calories and trying to keep germs off of all of my things in the middle of a building packed to the brim with hormonal teenagers."

"Yikes."

"Yeah, that about sums it up. But if he was the one who tattled on me, I owe him a great debt."

"Is that why you approached me in the church?" Chastity said like she'd just had a personal revelation. "Because you owed the Miller family a debt?"

"No, I owe Bradley a debt specifically. You, I dunno, I guessed I just sensed that you were hurting in a way that was familiar to me."

"You sure are something, Keiko."

She took another long sip of her coffee. "So, I've heard. But I believe we're here for shopping for intimates and other things, so how about that negligee store?"

She pointed at one of the entrances that was all done up with fancy curtains, and Sophia could smell the perfume from where she was. Chastity must have seen the expression on her face, because she steered Sophia in another direction. "How about a manicure first? We abuse our hands enough on the farm, might as well pamper them while we're here."

"I've never had a professional manicure before," Sophia said, spotting the nail place Chastity was steering her too. "Is it fun?"

"The good ones give you a nice massage," Missy said, coming up alongside them. "You know, Chastity was the one who took me to my first professional manicure too. I've been addicted ever since."

The dark-haired Chastity snorted. "Addicted? You get them once every three months and only when I'm in town."

"Doesn't mean I'm not addicted. I'm just busy."

Sophia let out a small breath, glad that she was rescued for a moment from the looming lingerie store. Suddenly, she was beginning to wonder if shopping was a bad idea.

Too late to back out now, she supposed.

THE MANICURE EXPERIENCE was actually nice. It was relaxing, and they really did give a great massage on her hands and even up her forearms. The only real downside of it was that she got a text on her phone and couldn't answer it until her hands sat under their weird UV light thing.

Oh yeah, Bradley had gotten her a new phone on his family's plan. She had fully intended on buying one of the nicer track phones out there but had been procrastinating. Having a phone was nice, but she also worried it was another way for her ex to hunt her down.

But then, one day, a package had been sitting for her on Bradley's couch when she went up to his office for lunch. She'd looked at him curiously, but he had pretended like it wasn't even there, the sly dog.

So now she had a shiny, very nice phone that was basically bigger than her hand. She had a new number, and she didn't have to worry about minutes or limits on texting or anything. She also didn't have to worry about any weird hacking mojo or police stuff considering the phone wasn't in her name, it was in the Miller's, and she doubted even her ex's father would have that much clout. The Millers were kind of a big deal, and she was only beginning to understand what that meant.

But in any case, having a phone meant being able to get texts, but she never really got any because the only people who had her number were the ones who she was around all the time anyway.

So curiosity ate at her more and more until finally, she was able to pull her phone out.

For a moment, she was afraid of the worst. But then she saw Bradley's name sitting there at the top of the message. He must have programmed it into the phone before she got it, because she hadn't put it in there yet.

How's THE SHOPPING GOING?

WASN'T that just the sweetest thing? The fact that he took the time to make sure she always had a way to talk to him made her heart melt in a ridiculous way. Geez, when had she become such a sap?

WE GOT OUR NAILS DONE.

HAHA, *of course. That's become Chastity's go to when out with the girls.*

BEFORE SHE COULD TYPE A RESPONSE, another text came through.

WHAT COLOR DID YOU PICK?

.   .   .

SHE SMILED GIDDILY to herself as she answered.

TAKE A WILD GUESS.

...PINK?

INSTEAD OF ANSWERING WITH WORDS, she held the phone out and took a pic of her nails in front of her smiling face.

YOU GOT IT!

THEY LOOK PRETTY.

SHE DIDN'T KNOW what possessed her, but she quickly typed out a response. *Do I look pretty?*

ALWAYS.

SHE COULDN'T STAND it anymore. She set her phone down so she could kick out her legs a little, clapping quietly to herself. But of course her actions didn't go unnoticed, and Dani sent her a curious look.

"Did you just get shocked, or something?"

"No, just happy thoughts."

"About your man?"

Sophia knew their whole thing was fake, she really did. But she still couldn't help but look down at her phone with glee. "Yeah."

"Good. You deserve to be happy. You know that, right?"

"Yeah, I'm finally starting to get that picture."

"You know, it took me a while too. To let my walls down, to trust people. But when I did, I got Benji, so believe me when I say it's worth it."

"Is it?"

Dani smiled serenely, and it was probably the first time Sophia had ever seen an expression like that on her. "Yeah. It really is."

Sophia took all of that in and turned it over in her head, sliding her phone back into her hoody pocket. And she kept on thinking about it as the rest of the girls finished up and they headed into the lingerie store.

But goodness, once they were inside of those walls, it was hard not to imagine wearing those skimpy and lacey things for Bradley. That made her feel a certain type of way that she hadn't in a long time. A heated, intense sort of longing filled her and made her thoughts go all sorts of ways that she wasn't used to.

Eventually, Missy noticed her discomfort and declared that three of the sets they had picked out for her were enough and took her to the bathing suit section. But then it was time for them to try *those* on over their underthings, and Sophia was suddenly subject to a very fleshy fashion show.

Geeze, all the women were so *beautiful*. It was no wonder why they'd caught the Miller brothers' eyes. Chastity was curvy with a soft little tummy that looked just right on her, her long hair framing her like some sort of princess.

And Missy? Missy was basically a classic bombshell, all curves and feminine with strong arms and muscle lines down her thick thighs.

Then there was Dani, who was exactly what all the boys she'd known back in the city would drool over. She had wide hips and a full backside that reminded her a lot of older art depicting women from long ago.

Then, finally, there was Keiko, the slender one of the group, and she looked like a porcelain doll. It didn't matter that she didn't have much cleavage or thick thighs. She was flawless, and it boggled Sophia's mind that the woman had once hated herself, once been so sick, that she couldn't even eat.

It was all so intimidating that she could only stand there in the changing room, three different one pieces laid out in front of her.

"You know, I can't believe the store has such a good plus-size selection," Dani said from the other side of the door. "Normally, I can only find this sort of stuff online."

"Yeah, this is one of the few stores that's pretty inclusive," Chastity said from a few stalls over. "It was always too expensive for me to go into before, but, yeah, you know how it is now."

"Times have certainly changed," Missy said. "Sometimes I catch myself doing something, and I marvel that two years ago, I never would have been able to even dream of anything like that."

"Yeah, the Millers are certainly a force of nature," Dani added, finally coming out of her stall. "Sometimes it feels like

I'm being swept up and I don't know *where* I'm going to end up."

"Yeah, but it's exciting, isn't it?"

"That's one way to put it.'

Sophia listened, her mind full, until someone knocked on her door.

"Hey," it was Missy's voice. "You okay in there."

"Yeah. I just, uh, I guess I'm feeling a little self-conscious."

"Aw, why? You're so pretty."

"Thanks. But I... I guess I don't feel that way right now. It's all a lot."

"Well, we're all changed back into our street clothes. Do you maybe just wanna catch some lunch instead?"

Sophia sighed gratefully, relief flooding her. "Yeah, I'd like that a lot."

"Oh, can we go to that Chinese place?" Keiko asked. "I swear, they have the fakest, most American food, but I love it so much."

Sophia hung the bathing suits on the hook of the door, still on their hangers. Swinging it open, she saw the four women looking at her with love and concern. That was right about when a thought hit her.

She had friends.

Real friends.

She'd had some when she was younger, but the last time she remembered having a crew she could hand out with was when she was seventeen.

That was a long time ago.

"Yeah, I could go for some mall Chinese food," she said.

They all headed together there as a group, and that feeling of belonging flooded her once more. Strange to think that it had only taken one brave man in a small-town inn to completely turn her life around.

She guessed fate was funny like that.

Thankfully, there wasn't a long line at any of the places in the food court, and they all scattered to find their favorites. Sophia, Keiko, and Dani all got the very American interpretation of Chinese food, while Chastity got some Tex-Mex and Missy loaded up on two burgers, fries, chicken nuggets, and a milkshake. Sophia had no idea where she put all of it. While Missy was broad with that Marilyn Monroe figure and biceps that looked like they could choke out a man, she wasn't rotund by any means.

But despite their separate taste, all of them joined up again and sat at one of the bigger tables. It was like the diner, only louder and with less emotional analyzing from Keiko. It was real nice, and Sophia felt her anxiety about the lingerie fade away.

Or at least, it did until Chastity was suddenly looking at her far too intensely.

"What?" Sophia asked, picking up a napkin and patting around her mouth to make sure she didn't have sesame sauce or something like that on her face.

"So, this thing with you and Bradley."

The hairs on the back of her neck stood up. "You mean our engagement?"

"Yeah. That."

She could tell that Chastity was trying to pick her words carefully, to not spook her, but that made Sophia tense up that much more. "What about it?"

"Is it real? Or is it just some sort of thing that's supposed to deter your ex?"

Huh, there it was. Out loud and in the open for everyone to know. Sophia had always thought that someone would eventually figure it out, but now that it happened, she could only stare at her food.

It had been so easy to pretend that what they had was real if no one else knew. To live in her little bubble of fake romance and charm. Now that someone else knew, everything was shattered to pieces in front of her.

"It's okay." Missy reached over to her, her larger hand resting over Sophia's. "I think the more important question is: do you want it to be real?"

Sophia was still for a long moment, her brain clamoring loudly. When she could eventually speak, her mouth was so dry that she had to take a few gulps of her soda.

"Yeah, it is. And yes, I do. Is that... stupid of me?"

"How could it be stupid?"

"It's stupid because I've been running from a man since I was twenty, and I've fallen in love with the first man I've had prolonged contact with that isn't my ex. And if it's not stupid, then maybe it's desperate. Or naïve. Or, I dunno, *something*."

"No, honey. No, it's not." Chastity reached forward too, her hands resting over Missy's. It was a little stack of sisterly support, and Sophia could feel herself tear up already.

Geez, when had she gotten so sappy? *He* would have never allowed it. He couldn't stand tears. Said that they were a weapon to manipulate him.

But she didn't have to worry about stuff like that anymore. She was safe.

Keiko's voice was kind as she draped her arm over Sophia's shoulders. But then again, when wasn't she kind?

"I've known Bradley for a long time, and we both read books because we were looking for something that we were missing. Things we found in the pages that weren't in the real world. He looks at you the same way he would look at a really good book. Like it was exactly what he was missing, and he finally found it. That's not something you can fake."

"I don't know about that..."

"I do. Trust me. I'm good at reading people."

Sophia managed a faint chuckle. "Yeah, I have first-hand experience of that."

A snapping sound drew Sophia's attention, and her gaze automatically flicked to Dani. The normally pale woman was a bright and angry red. The plastic fork in her hand was snapped right in two, that must have been where the sound came from, but her gaze was decidedly over Sophia's shoulder.

"What...?"

"We should go," she said firmly. "We should go *right now*."

"Whoa, Dani. What bee got up in your bonnet?"

But Sophia knew. She didn't want to believe it, but deep down, she knew exactly what Dani was looking at that way.

Or rather, *who.*

She jumped to her feet, grabbing her purse and bags to race off, but then *he* called out to her.

"Sophie!"

She froze in place, her heart hammering in her chest. For a moment, she had no idea what to do and she just stood there.

But unlike all those other times, she wasn't alone. All four of the women made a protective circle around her, tensed like they were ready for battle.

Because that's what it was, wasn't it? A battle. Her nemesis, her mortal enemy, had finally showed up for the confrontation that she'd managed to dodge for so long.

"I'm calling the police!" Chastity said. They were starting to get looks from the other folks in the place, but none of the women seemed to care. Her ex really must have been desperate, to try to approach her in such a public place. "You stay there!"

"I have a right to see my own fiancé!"

Suddenly something snapped within Sophia, and a fire blazed within her. Or maybe that fire had always been there and she just had never given it enough fuel to become the inferno it wanted to be.

"I am *not* your fiancé!" she cried, whirling to him. She was so tired of running. Of being scared. Of acting like an animal that was being hunted by some big, bad predator.

Unlike he'd always tried to make her believe, Sophia knew she wasn't actually weak. She wasn't useless. She was a *woman* and a human and so many things.

"You do not own me. Nor do you have any say in what I do. Do you understand me?" she stepped out of the protective circle of her friends; voice raised.

He actually had the gall to look surprised for a moment, but he quickly recovered.

Sophia clenched her fists at her side. "You are nothing to me but a bad memory. So get out of here and leave me alone!"

He advanced on her, just like she guessed he would. "Being around all these rich folks has messed with your head. They've confused you, gotten your thoughts all twisted up. But you know you don't belong in this world with them. They'll just keep you around as long as you're a novelty and then pitch you out like always."

He took a step towards her, trying to play up that charm that had first taken her in. But she had someone in her life who was *actually* charming, so she saw through him like glass.

Her ex continued talking, spewing his lies, "Come on now, Sophia, who's always been there for you? Protected you? Provided for you? I'm the only one who understands you, keeps you out of trouble."

"You *beat* me!" she screamed. But it felt good to scream. Three years together and she never raised her voice at the monster standing in front of her. It felt like she was long over-due. "You terrorized me! You made me feel *small!* But no more. That's over! And you better leave before the cops get here, because I guarantee you even your daddy can't get you out of this scot-free if they arrest you."

He wasn't used to this side of her, the side that he had muted so long ago. His face flushed red, and before she knew it, his fist was flying towards her. Before she would have just flinched away or curled into a wall and begged him to stop, apologizing over and over again.

But times had changed, and so had she.

So many things happened at once. Her friends surged forward, various protests or warnings coming from them. People in the food court jumped up, some moving to run away, others coming forward.

As for Sophia, she settled her feet back into the stance that Missy had shown her and brought her arm across her body in one swift motion, deflecting his punch. And then, while he still had all his momentum put into his missed blow, she slugged him in the nose as hard as she could.

There was a popping sound that was either his face or her knuckle, and an explosion of pain in her hand, but he stumbled back, holding his nose. Blood was leaking out between his fingers, and Sophia had never been so satisfied at repeating one of Missy's lessons.

"I *said* to leave. Now. I'm done with you, Travis." She advanced on him; fists raised in case he tried again. "You don't have any power over me anymore.

"You know why? Because I'm worthy of love. I'm worthy of good things. You're wrong, and you always have been." She was almost to his face, his brows furrowed as he stared at her incredulously. "You're a coward, Travis, and I pity you. Get out of my sight."

And in that moment, it was like a weight was lifted off her. Like shackles were removed from her wrists, her neck, and her heart.

Yeah, she was going to still have to see her therapist, and no, she wasn't cured of all her issues. But she had stared her greatest fear in the face and then punched it. A whole new era of her life was opening up right in front of her, starting with the demise of the man who so delighted in torturing her.

But of course, *he* couldn't leave well enough alone. Standing up to his full height, his eyes roved behind her. She guessed that he saw the mall cops that were no doubt starting to respond to the commotion. He was going to run at any moment, because while he was big and strong, he also could never face the consequences of his actions. Like she said, he was a coward.

With one last sneer, he spit at her feet. "You're not worth the effort anyway."

"See, wrong again, Travis. I'm worth so much more than you will ever know."

He looked like he wanted to argue with her. Like he wanted to try to cut her down again, but she could hear the cops calling out for him to calm down and put his hands up.

"You better run now," she warned, letting him know exactly what she thought of him.

He turned on his heel and ran out, blood streaked down his face. Sophia stood there, watching him until he was out of the glass doors.

Abruptly, she was surrounded by her friends and they were all talking at once.

"Oh my gosh, Sophia, that was amazing!"

"You did it! You really slugged him in the face!"

"Are you alright? Is your hand okay? Holy cow, Sophia!"

"I knew you could do it. I knew you were ready to stand up to him. I'm so proud of you. We all are!"

They looked like they wanted to say so much more, but then the mall cops were herding them to the first aid station and asking so many questions.

It was all sort of a haze around Sophia, her adrenaline fading as the reality of what happened settled in. She had done it. She had faced down Travis and told him off. Suddenly, those shadows were gone. She'd chased off the boogeyman.

But then, a singular voice called her name, and all of the world came back in brilliant clarity.

"*Sophia!*"

She turned, wresting her arm from the mall cops to see Bradley standing at the entrance, looking terrified and relieved all at once.

"Bradley?"

"What happened?" He dropped the bouquet of flowers that was in his hand. "I just wanted to surprise y—"

He never got the sentence fully out. But that was probably because Sophia bolted towards him, throwing her arms around his shoulders and hauling herself up for a kiss.

Because finally, she knew what she wanted, and she wasn't afraid to get it.

And she wanted Bradley more than anything else in the world.

21

Bradley

*S*uddenly his arms were full of Sophia.

He wasn't complaining, however, and he nearly crushed her to him as her lips met his, hungrily demanding his attention. So many thoughts and feelings were rushing through him, he felt like he might up and float away if he didn't have her as an anchor to the ground they were standing on.

Bradley hadn't intended to come to the mall when his day started. It wasn't like he felt the need to constantly check in on Sophia, after all, she was a grown woman and could do what she wanted. But Sophia had been so adorable when they were texting that he couldn't concentrate on his work. So he figured that she wouldn't mind it too much if he crashed the end of her mall outing and brought her some flowers.

After all, they'd been "together" for quite a while, and he

had never gotten her any before. There was definitely something wrong with that, so he decided it was the time to remedy the situation.

Thankfully, Missy was giving him text updates on how their day was going. Without his even asking, she'd texted him a couple of times throughout the day to tell him things were going well, and when they were going to get food. When she had mentioned *what* stores they were visiting... well, it was hard to keep his mind off of that. Of course, Missy knew that. She was just as insightful as Keiko, but a bit more subdued about it.

When he'd arrived at the mall, coming in the main doors to the food court, he was nearly shoulder-checked by a man in a great hurry to leave.

Bradley had been so concerned with not dropping his phone or the flowers that he didn't even think about who had nearly tackled him for at least a solid couple of seconds. But then a belated flash of recognition shot through him, and he whirled just in time to see a large man jump into his jeep and race off.

Wait... did he know that guy? His mind scrolled through faces like an old-fashioned Rolodex until it clicked.

No. It couldn't be.

Nearly dropping the flowers again, he rushed inside only to see Sophia was there, alright, but being escorted away by some mall cops.

So many feelings flooded him that for a second, he shorted out. He was shocked, confused, and definitely worried, but also immensely relieved. She was fine. She was in front of him, and healthy and then she was flying through the air and smashing her lips to his.

All of that had happened so fast, but he wasn't complaining. No, he was doing the exact opposite of that. Or at least he would be if his mouth wasn't busy with Sophia.

Some sort of barrier between them was broken, and everything he had been holding back was pouring out. How could he be taking advantage when kissing her brought so much joy? When her pressed to him made the world seem right?

Eventually, however, they had to break for air. Besides that night in the truck, it had been a long while since he'd kissed anyone, and he got the feeling he needed to work on his technique a little.

He set Sophia down gently, holding her face in his hands and just looking at her. Memorizing her. Burning her into his memory like the work of art that she was.

She was so... perfect.

She pressed her face into his palms, and there was so much he wanted to ask her. If she was alright, if touching her like this was okay. If maybe, if maybe she had even a fraction of the same feelings for him as he had for her.

They stayed like that for not nearly long enough, until eventually her own hand came up to cup his. But then she winced, and it jerked him from the moment.

"What's wrong?"

"Nothing," she said quickly. Which meant exactly the opposite of nothing.

"Let me see."

Gently he took her hand and looked at it. A couple of her knuckles were swollen and already starting to bruise. "We should really go to the ER. I think this might be broken."

"Excuse me, sir. Do you know this woman?"

Oh right, they were surrounded by mall cops.

"Yes, she's my fiancé, and we're going to the hospital."

"The police are on their way. They're going to need to ask some questions."

"Then they can come ask them at the hospital." He looked to the rest of their friends. "You'll all stay here and tell them whatever they need, right?"

"Yeah, of course."

"Sir, you can't just—"

"Uh...yes I can."

Normally, Bradley was all about respect and treating service individuals with patience and politeness, but he was out of both when it came to anything standing between him and taking care of Sophia.

Turning to her, he swept her up in a bridal carry. She let out a surprised squeak, but he was happy when she curled into him rather than shrinking away. The mall cops didn't try to stop him, and he kicked open one of the doors to go to his truck.

"You know, you dropped the flowers in there."

"I'll buy you new ones," he said with a chuckle, not setting her down until he was at the truck. "Lots and lots of them."

"Bradley, I'm not a cripple. My hand just hurts."

"Maybe I just want to carry you. I kind of like it. Is that so wrong?"

"Well, no." She let him open the door for her but climbed in herself. He was about to go around when he noticed she was having a bit of trouble buckling in her seatbelt. "Ok, ya, maybe I could use a *little* help."

"That's what I'm here for."

Leaning over her carefully, he clicked the buckle into the latch before shutting her door. He felt like he was going to vibrate out of his skin as he went around the car. Jumping in, he peeled out of the parking lot, only slowing down after reminding himself that there were pedestrians and he needed to be careful.

But it was hard to be careful when he thought of Sophia hurting.

"So, do you want to tell me what happened? Or do you need a few minutes to process through it first?" he said as he plugged the hospital address into his GPS. He knew the general way from the couple of times he drove Dani's brothers to checks ups and physical therapy back when Benji had the flu, but he didn't want to waste time accidentally making the wrong turn.

"Well, as I'm sure you figured out, my ex showed up."

Bradley's hands tightened on the wheel. "Did he hit you?" The thought made his temperature skyrocket. If that man so much as—

"Nope. I mean, well he tried to, but I blocked it with a move Missy showed me, and then I socked him right in that stupid nose of his."

If Bradley wasn't driving through busy city streets, he would have turned and stared at her.

But that didn't stop him from glancing at her a few times over his arm. "You *punched* him?"

She beamed at him, proud as could be. "I sure did. That's how I hurt my hand. I must have not held my fist how Missy told me to, but I don't mind. It's worth it."

Bradley's mind almost bugged out with a thousand thoughts. She *punched* her ex? She *punched* her ex. Right in the face!

Sure, it was a bit concerning that her ex was watching her enough to know when she would be away from Bradley and the Ranch, and that he had approached her in a public place, but she had *punched her ex in the face!*

That was huge.

First of all, it made him so proud of her he thought the feeling might burst right through his chest. Secondly, it made him wonder if she wasn't scared of him anymore. If that sort of heavy presence he could see weighing on her sometimes would finally wane, and she would be freer than she had ever been.

He wondered if he had been part of the reason she was strong enough to do that. If his help had given her a place to heal and discover who she was. That... that was a very nice thought to have.

And finally, if she had faced down her ex, if she had slugged him across the face like he deserved, made him less of a bogeyman and more just a pitiful man... did that mean she was ready to move on? To maybe... possibly have something real with him?

"I can't believe you hauled off and punched him. I wish I had been there to see it. Or that I'd been there to fight him. Wouldn't mind getting in a few hits myself."

"I mean, I wouldn't mind watching you absolutely pummel him—I think he's really scared of you—but it needed to be me."

The steel in her voice was audible even over all the sounds of traffic. She really was something, this beautiful, strong woman beside him.

"Why's that?"

"Because I've let him rule over too much of my life. Influence too many of my thoughts and how I lived my life. I needed to be the one who drew the line in the sand and told him that wasn't happening anymore." She reached over with her unhurt left hand. "But just so you know, you're the one who gave me all the tools to do it. Well, I mean your whole family did. But you most of all."

"I..." Bradley swallowed. Those were exactly the words that he had wanted to hear. Exactly what he had hoped she'd say, so it was a bit uncanny to hear them out loud and in the open.

"Did I?" he said for the lack of anything better to say. Not for the first time, he wished that he was as good with words as he was with numbers.

"Yeah." Her fingers squeezed his palm before interlacing with his own digits. "You showed me that it was alright to love myself. That I wasn't all the things my ex said I was. And you showed me that even if I was afraid, even if I've got all these wounds—either on the inside or out—I can still have a life. That there are things to look forward to and dream about and, and a *future*. For the first time since I was seventeen, I can see a glimmer of a future there. And that's all because of you."

Wow. That was certainly a lot. "I don't know if I did all that," he said, although he was practically glowing at the same time. He thought back to that first night that he had met Sophia, when she was shaking and bruised and snapping. When she snapped that she wasn't weak as if to convince herself more than him. How she'd refused any help and thought there wasn't a point to even trying to prosecute her ex.

What a change. What a beautiful, perfect change.

Happiness filled his entire body, more than it ever did at the end of a long horseback ride, or the end of a good book, or even when finding out that one of his investments was returning even more than he calculated. Seeing Sophia grow and heal, it was hands down the biggest accomplishment he had achieved in his entire life. He would take it to his grave proud and content.

Well, maybe not content. Because when he glanced over at Sophia, seeing her sitting there all happy and excited, looking at her busted hand like it was a trophy, he realized he wanted more than their fake arrangement. He wanted more than a bubble that they both escaped to every so often. And for the first time since he'd admitted his feelings, he thought that she might feel the same.

They pulled into the hospital, and this time he was able to park. It was a vast difference from the previous time when she had been rushed directly in by an ambulance. Together, they walked in—she refused to let him carry her through the doors like he wanted to—and she walked up to the nurse at the front desk.

The nurse looked up at them. "Hi, how may I help you?"

Sophia held up her hand. "Uh, had a bit of an accident. And by accident, I mean I punched someone in the face."

To the woman's credit, she just nodded calmly and handed Sophia a clipboard. "Are you able to write?"

"Not really, but my fiancé will do it for me."

She handed the paper to Bradley, and he tried not to preen that she was still using the word 'fiancé' to describe him. The threat of her ex was over, she had said as much herself, but she didn't seem very eager to end their charade.

"Oh, and some cops are probably going to be here in a few minutes, and they're going to want to ask some questions. Also, you might get a warning about a guy coming in to be treated for a busted face, but I don't think he'll show his face around here since I humiliated him in public."

The woman blinked at Sophia, still collected. "Alright. Is there anything else that I should know?"

"Well, I'm an Aries and I'm righthanded, but that's about it."

"Alright, have a seat. You'll be called back shortly."

Bradley couldn't help but chuckle at Sophia's whole demeanor. It was like she was floating, high on her own adrenaline but not in a self-destructive way. He liked seeing her like this and wondered if this was going to be more of her new normal.

Wouldn't that be something?

Thankfully, it seemed to be a slow day in the ER, because they only had to wait about a half hour to be seen. Pretty impressive for her relatively mild injury. The nurses took her in alone for a while, and he knew they were asking her if she was in an abusive relationship, if he had been the one who hurt her, and if she needed help, along with taking x-rays and the like. He didn't mind, however. Questions were good. Questions were how victims got help.

But after a while, a nurse came and got him and said he could wait with Sophia in her room. He followed her back, but barely had time to sit down and pull her good hand into his grip before a couple of cops came in.

"Miss Hernandez?" one of them asked. Bradley was pretty sure it was the same two they had met the first time she was in the ER.

"That's me."

"We heard you had a run in with a man at the local mall."

"You heard right. That was my ex, the one who put me here the last time."

"Ah. And we also heard he fled the scene with blood on his face."

"Did he? Wow, that's so sad."

"And your hand was injured at the mall."

"I know, that's crazy, right?"

Bradley wasn't sure what to think of Sophia's borderline flippant attitude. It was better than the shaking, upset, and desperate dismissal she had yelled at them before, but it was still pretty... cheeky. And city cops weren't like the amiable chaps down in town.

"Ma'am, we looked it up and saw that you have three different restraining orders against one Travis Wilcox, as well as plenty of evidence as to why those restraining orders were filed. So, if he was there, he was in gross violation of all three of them."

"Yeah, it was definitely a gross violation. But it's taken care of now. I used some good old fashioned self-defense to show him the door."

"That's... that's good ma'am. We're glad you were able to de-escalate the situation."

Bradley was surprised when one of the cops sat down opposite him on the other side of the bed. "But if he violated the terms of your restraining order, that means he broke the law. It's our jurisdiction, and my partner and I have a feeling that maybe, if we dug a little, we'd find a whole lot more that he might have done."

"Oh, that's a good idea," Sophia said brightly. "Because I want to press charges."

It took a while for Sophia to tell her whole story and answer all the cops' questions. The nurses then put a wrist brace on her. She did apparently fracture one of her metacarpals and would have to baby it for a couple weeks, which meant no commissions, but Bradley was fine with that. He was going to swaddle her with blankets and comforts and spoil her so rotten that she forgot what it was like to ever want for anything.

Or at least something like that.

When she was signing the last of her forms with her left hand, Bradley went and got the truck from the parking garage so that he could pick her up at the ER doors. That same feeling of excitement, of all those possibilities, bubbled up inside of him as he waited for her to come outside.

When she eventually did, he all but vaulted from his truck, going around to open her door and help her in. This time, she didn't have to ask him to buckle her seatbelt for her, and then he was closing her door and going back around.

When he got in, he didn't want to drive away immediately. There was too much on his mind, too many things threatening to boil over into a bubbling mess.

"Something wrong?" Sophia asked, looking over him curiously as he idled in front of the ER entrance.

"No, I just. I..." Turning to her, he took her good hand in one of his, his other reaching out to stroke the side of her face. She was so *soft*. So warm. He didn't think he would ever tire of the contact and how it made so *much* rush through him. "I was just wondering if maybe, you'd like to date for real."

"Oh, Bradley," she murmured, smiling brightly at him even as her eyes started to water. "I think we've been dating for a while and were just trying to deny it because that was a little bit scary."

His eyes widened at that. "You mean it was real to you too?"

She nodded. "Ever since you took me out of that jail, yeah."

Bradley had to breathe for just a moment, the ramifications of everything she was saying rushing through him. Sophia felt the same as he did. And the way she was looking at him made him want to dance, throw something really far, and write out a brand-new math equation all at once.

He didn't think it was possible, but she was right in front of him, saying that he wasn't crazy. That he wasn't taking advantage.

"I think I love you, Miss Sophia Hernandez."

"Well, that's good," she said with the slightest of chuckles. "Considering we're engaged and all."

He couldn't stand being apart from her for another breath. He closed in, pressing his lips to her, tentatively at first, but growing in pressure.

Once more she melted to him, her small form pushing against his as her arms wrapped around his shoulders. He had no idea what he had done to deserve such an amazing, strong, and brilliant woman in his life, but he was done second-guessing.

It made him dizzy to think that she wanted to be with him too, and that made him press her to him all the more. It was overwhelming and amazing, and everything he wanted all at once.

HONK!

They both jumped and quickly pulled apart. Oh, right. They were in the middle of the drive leading away from the ER entrance. They should probably get a move on.

"We're being a little inconsiderate," Sophia said with a chuckle.

"Yeah," he agreed, turning the car on. "But this isn't over. We have a lot to talk about when we get home."

"Why do I get the feeling that's not all we'll be doing?"

"Probably because I'm going to kiss you, and not stop until we can't breathe anymore."

"Huh, that could be fun, I think."

"I'm up for it."

"Promises, promises."

"Hey, the way I figure it, we have lost time to make up for."

"Bradley, my life's been nothing but lost time since I was seventeen. I fully intend to spend the rest of it living to the fullest. After all, I'm only twenty-two."

"Especially if I have anything to say about it," Bradley agreed.

"Stick around and you definitely will."

"Trust me, I'm not going anywhere."

Once more her hand reached out to rest on his. "And you know what? I believe that. I really do."

He wanted to lean over and kiss her again, but that wouldn't exactly be prudent considering he was at the wheel. So instead, he put on the CD from the musical he had taken her to. It didn't take long for her to start singing. And it was hand in hand that they finally drove back home.

To *their* home.

For real.

EPILOGUE

Sophia

Sophia filed into the court rows with the rest of the Millers in front and behind her. They made up quite the clan, but even they weren't the only ones on her side of the seating.

True to their word, the cops had done some digging after they'd talked to her, and in the months that passed afterward, they uncovered quite a lot.

First of all, Travis hadn't always been Travis. Before her, he'd been Deacon. Before that, John. Apparently, he changed his name whenever he changed states, and he changed states those two times because he had outstanding warrants for assaults in each of them.

His father had tried his best to cover them up, using all of his connections, but the cops had been determined. They had found the loose ends, and those loose ends lead them to two other women who each had experience with Deacon and John.

With Travis.

Apparently, he targeted younger girls. The first had been just sixteen when he'd whisked her off on a whirlwind romance. She ended up running away from home, and he carted her over several counties. It took her two years to get free, and only because her parents were able to file a kidnapping charge, so he had to run.

With the next girl, he had learned. He told her to keep their relationship a secret. They were together for three whole years before she got away. And she'd made her escape only because she'd had an 'accident' severe enough that she was stuck in the hospital for a month, and the cops were investigating even without her pressing charges.

Their names were Michelle and Kim, and the two of them sat right behind her as she returned to her spot at the plaintiff's table. He liked to go after young girls of color. Her attorney said it was because they were the least likely to get help or be taken seriously, and the most likely to already be disadvantaged in some way. She wasn't sure what to think of that. She had always thought that she just had the bad luck of running into the wrong man at the wrong time, but finding out that he was specifically looking for a girl like her, poor, from a large family, on the edge of graduating high school. She'd been targeted and then stalked.

They all had.

In her opinion, the man needed to rot in prison for all eternity, but her lawyers explained that was unlikely to happen. Laws were funny that way. Although he had done terrible, terrible things to each of them, the statute of limitations had long since passed for the two of them in both of their states, so all of it was on Sophia.

Despite that, the women had agreed to testify to show a history of abuse. Of a dangerous pattern that had to be stopped. And after three weeks of grueling trials, maybe it actually was going to.

She looked over her shoulder, her eyes scanning for Bradley in the crowd. Of course, he was there, right next to Michelle and Kim, shaking with barely withheld rage.

But when their eyes melt, she watched his anger melt away. There was only love in his eyes for her. And a sort of admiration she didn't think she deserved. But Bradley was also like that, giving her more than she could ever ask for then acting like it was never enough.

She never would have gotten through the two-year process of everything coming together without him. Sure, there had been bright points, like Dani and Benji's wedding, and even Keiko finding someone, but there had been a whole lot of stress too.

And finally, finally, she would learn if all of that was worth it.

After everyone settled, the jurors all filed in, somber and silent. When they were fully seated, the bailiff entered, the judge, and finally Travis.

He was dressed in a suit, but she thought he would have looked better in an orange jumpsuit. It was best she not get ahead of herself though. The DA had made it quite clear to her that domestic violence trials could often be terribly messy and involve a hung jury at the end—and that apparently wasn't a term that meant they were all dead.

And the defense hadn't exactly made it easy. They'd

blocked a lot of evidence and really tried to sell Travis' character, painting him as a good guy and her as some manipulating gold digger who purposefully triggered him, set him up, then ran off when she found a richer target. She hadn't wanted him to, but her attorney had called Bradley to the stand to testify about their relationship, and how they had met, and she hoped that was enough to counteract any of the jury that might have been swayed by their sob story.

"Jury, have you reached a verdict?"

"Yes, we have," one of the jurors in the corner of their pen stood up, a piece of paper in her hands.

"In the case of the state of Montana versus John T. Wilcox, we came to a unanimous decision on the following charges:

"On the charge of stalking in violation of a protection order, we find John T. Wilcox guilty."

A ripple went right through Sophia's soul. Guilty. *Guilty.* She wanted to get up and shout, to do a cartwheel. Any victory was a victory, after all, but the juror was still talking.

"On the charge of illegal surveillance, we find John T. Wilcox guilty."

She could feel the energy of the women behind her and wished she could turn and hold their hands. Two wins. And with each one, she could see Travis wilt that much more.

Good. For once he couldn't run away from his punishment. He'd lived his whole life getting away with using and abusing others. Now he was going to be locked up until he learned how to not be a monster.

The juror continued, though, "And in the case of his third offense, assault on a partner, due to John T. Wilcox's history and multiple orders of protection with two other young women, and his connections that have allowed him to evade the law so far, we consider him guilty. We suggest the full penalty under the law."

"Thank you, jury. You are dismissed."

And there it was.

They won.

This time Sophia did let out a cry, jumping to her feet. The attorney stood and went to shake the defense's hand, but Sophia had no desire to do that. She looked to Travis, who was just standing there, looking shocked.

Everything was a blur for a moment, with hugs and tears and claps and congratulations. Michelle and Kim especially clung to her, thanking her over and over again for doing what they couldn't.

But Sophia didn't feel like she deserved that much credit. They were basically all on their own when they escaped, and younger than her. She had the entire Miller clan on her side. And that was certainly a force to be reckoned with.

Eventually, however, they were asked to go out in the hall. But as soon as they were there, Bradley swept her up, swinging her around in a circle and pressing a kiss to both of her cheeks and finally her mouth.

She kissed him back with just as much relief. She couldn't believe it. Her nightmare was over. She'd lived through actual hell, walked through the fire, and she had come out the other side.

Thank the Lord.

"Hey, you can't hog her all to yourself!" Ma said, tapping Bradley on the shoulder. The two of them laughed, and he put her down just in time for more hugs from more people.

By the time it slowed down, she was pretty sure that she'd at least embraced everyone twice, even Pa, and she was beginning to feel a little worn, thirsty, and rough around the edges.

"So," Dani said, grabbing her hand. "Now that this is all finally out of the way, are you finally gonna think about your wedding colors, or are you still gonna foist that off on Bradley?"

"Pink and gray," she said without hesitation.

Missy laughed from beside their shorter friend. "Wow, it sounds like you might have been thinking about this stuff after all."

"Maybe from time to time. How could I not? But it's not like I have a binder of clippings or anything."

"No," Bradley said, slinging his arm over her shoulders. "She wrote it down in this little silver notebook, actually."

Sophia looked at him, a smile on her face. "Bradley has some terrific ideas too. He's very good at making wedding decisions."

Truthfully, she wasn't interested in spending a lot of money on a wedding or having a big, frilly white dress or a group of girls to stand beside her in overly expensive dresses. To her, the most important part was the *reception*, where everyone got together and danced and ate and gave silly speeches. Now that seemed like the real magic to her. The kind of thing that made her heart warm, fuzzy, and full.

"Oh well. To be honest, after the stress of this, I'm not sure I'll ever have enough energy to deal with that whole ceremony and the pomp and circumstance. I wish we could bypass that part and vault to the reception and honeymoon."

"Is that so?" Bradley said.

Something was off about his tone, so she twisted to look up at his face. But his eyes weren't on her at all, but rather on a sign behind her.

"What are you looking at?"

"A possibility," he said, pulling her closer to it.

When she was close enough to finally see, she understood exactly what he meant.

"Really? You'd want to do that here, and now?"

"Why not?"

"Ma is gonna be furious."

"Nah, I have a plan for her. So what do you say?"

Sophia looked at the sign in front of them, the one that had two simple words and an arrow.

Marriage Licenses.

"I guess I say I do."

"I think that part's for later." He leaned down and gave her a peck on the cheek. "Stay right here. I have to go break the news to Ma and herd the rest of them out of here. Who do you want as your witness?"

"Uh, Missy, I guess. You don't think that'll hurt anyone's feelings, will it?"

"Nah. They've got plenty to do. Here," he guided her over to a bench. "Just sit tight."

There was something strange about the way he was carrying himself, but she guessed it was probably excitement. Or maybe even relief. Bradley didn't seem into all the finery and complications of a massive wedding either.

They really were a perfect match.

But she didn't get time by herself to muse over it for long, because soon Missy joined her. Sophia understood that a *huge* thing had just happened, but the woman seemed chattier than usual, asking all sorts of questions about everything from her plans on what to do next, if Michelle and Kim were going to stay for a while, and if she ever thought about getting a dog or some other pet. In fact, she managed to pretty much keep a constant stream of dialogue going, which Sophia answered dutifully.

She was so busy answering question after question, that she didn't realize how much time had passed until Bradley came jogging back to them.

"Where were you?" she asked. "That was about twenty minutes?"

"Sorry, people love to chitchat. You know how it is."

"I suppose." But her irritation faded as he offered her his arm.

"Are you ready?"

"As I'll ever be."

He grinned, and together they headed in the direction the arrow pointed them to, Missy right behind them.

But it turned out that it didn't matter if she was ready or not, because once they reached the right floor, they had to stand in line for a half hour. And that was just to *get* the papers that they needed to sign. Apparently, people were supposed to schedule these sorts of things ahead of time, but they lucked out that there were a few evening slots that had been canceled, so they might have *just* enough time to fill out the papers and stand in the *other* line to turn them in.

"We're not going to get out of here until after seven," Sophia groaned.

"Huh, well that's perfect."

"What do you mean by that?"

Bradley shrugged, his classic move, and it was Missy who answered.

"Because that means we'll miss rush hour. I don't know about you, but the three of us in a truck, stuck in traffic doesn't sound like a great way to spend part of your wedding night."

"Ah, that makes sense." Sophia thought for a moment. "You know, maybe we shouldn't go straight home. Maybe we should, like, get tacos or something."

"Yeah, you know tacos do sound kinda nice," Bradley said.

Sophia flashed him a happy grin as she went about filling out the paperwork. She had never thought at the start of the day that she would see her abuser get his just desserts *and* marry the love of her life, but it seemed that she was just blessed that day. Maybe later they could have an actual ceremony. But first, since the trial was finally over, maybe they could skip right to the honeymoon.

Her cheeks flushed, and she wrote faster.

Unsurprisingly, Bradley finished first and helped her with the rest of hers. From there, they got into the other line, and the rest of it went exactly how the first clerk said it would.

Missy did her best to keep them both distracted and entertained, telling them funny stories from the vet's office she worked at in town. Before Sophia knew it, their papers were in and they just had to wait another half hour to be seen.

Although that half hour probably would have gone by a lot less anxiously if Bradley wasn't constantly texting on his phone.

"Who are you even talking to?" she asked when his phone buzzed for about the dozenth time in ten minutes.

"Sorry, just getting chewed out by Ma. It's worth it though, don't worry."

"I didn't think she could text that fast." Sophia knew she

couldn't. She'd seen the woman try to type a couple of times and it was a near painful experience.

"Well, she can't. But my brothers are all asking me if I really had to upset her when it was already a pretty exhausting day and Dani is asking if she should pack so we could head off on our honeymoon right away."

"Are you telling her that we haven't even picked a honeymoon destination yet?"

"I'm telling her I have it handled."

Weird answer, but it satisfied her curiosity, and then Missy was pulling her to the bathroom to put lipstick on her and zhuzh up her hair. By the time they came back, they only sat down for a minute before their names were called.

She couldn't believe it. It was really happening.

"So, are you ready to be a Mrs.?" Bradley asked as they walked through the judge's doors.

"I thought you'd never ask."

THE WHOLE PROCESS turned out to be a lot easier than she thought. The judge asked them to state their names and their intent to marry. He asked their witness to state her name as well, and then the judge was explaining some things, and then he asked Bradley if he wanted to take her as his wife.

Yeah, it really was that quick and easy apparently. Even Bradley seemed a little surprised. "Going kinda fast there, aren't ya?"

"I've been here since six am. I want to go home to my family. Now, if you don't mind, do you take this woman to be your lawfully wedded wife?"

"Uh, I do. Yeah, of course. I do."

"And do you, take this man to be your lawfully wedded husband?"

"I do!"

"Good. Then sign on this line."

That wasn't exactly what Sophia had been expecting, and she faltered for a moment. But Bradley recovered, taking the pen from the judge and signing the certificate, then Sophia signing after him, then finally Missy signing as the witness.

When they stood, Bradley looked at the judge expectantly.

"What?" the judge asked.

"Uh, aren't you forgetting something?" Bradley said.

"What? Oh. Right. You may kiss the bride."

And boy did he.

Both of his strong arms wrapped around her back, pulling her close to him as he claimed her mouth. It was heady and deep and made her soul practically leave her body.

When they parted, she was nearly dizzy from it all and let out a giddy laugh.

"Well, hello there, Mrs. Miller."

"You know, there's a whole lot of us now," Missy remarked from behind them, smiling broadly. "It's getting confusing."

"That's right," Sophia said. "All the brothers ringed up but one now, and I have a feeling that's just a matter of time."

"Oh, do you now?"

"Uh-huh."

"You may go," the judge said shooing them towards the exit, prompting them all to leave.

So they did just that, heading all the way downstairs and towards the exit onto the street. But before they made it, Sophia saw Dani rushing up to them, a long thin package in her hand.

"Hey, what are you doing here?" she asked.

But Dani didn't answer, instead just grabbing her hand and pulling her along. "Let's go to the bathroom."

"Wait, what?"

But her questions were ignored until they were in the restroom and Dani shoved the box into Sophia's arms. Carefully, she opened it, but what she saw inside was pretty confusing.

"Why are you handing me a dress?"

"Well, what do you normally do with dresses?"

"Dani, what's—"

"Just put it on! Come on, trust me. I'm one of your girls, right?"

The whole situation was really, really weird, but Sophia went with it, taking the dress into one of the stalls. It didn't take her long to get out of the simple, court appropriate outfit she was in and slide into the gown, but she did have to call Dani in to lace up the back for her.

It was a beautiful dress, pearl-encrusted on the front and fitted all the way down to her knees where it flared out in a sudden rush of beautiful chiffon. It was that same dusky pink that she preferred to wear whenever there was a fancy event, and there was delicate silver-gray embroidery around the waist, bust, and translucent sleeves.

Sophia didn't really have much in the way of curves, but the way the dress sat on her made her feel so womanly. It reminded her a lot of all the bookmarks she had saved to her computer, as well as the drawings she'd made in her wedding idea notebook.

Well, it was her wedding day. Maybe Bradley had swung some things around to try to get her the perfect dress for tacos.

It was silly, but also incredibly wonderful. It was just like him to surprise her with something so thoughtful.

"There you go," Dani said when she was all laced up. "My, you look so beautiful, you know that?"

"Yeah," Sophia said, this time with confidence. "I do."

But when she opened the handicapped stall that they were in, she was surprised to see Chastity waiting there with what looked like a very full makeup case and lots of hair styling supplies.

"Are you ready to get glammed up?" she said, wiggling one of the makeup brushes.

"Guys, I don't think this is necessary."

"Shh, shh, shh, you stand here by the sink in the good light and let me do what I'm gonna do. Trust me."

"You know, I'm hearing that a lot the past few minutes, and I'm getting a little suspicious."

"Huh, isn't that something."

But Sophia still did as her friend asked, standing under the light and letting her do her makeup. About fifteen minutes later, she was finally walking out of the bathroom.

Only to see Bradley standing in the middle of the entryway in a silver tux, a dusky pink vest beneath and a dark gray shirt. Sophia's jaw dropped, and suddenly she understood.

"Bradley..." she murmured, walking towards him. "This is the wedding. Like I drew in my book."

"Maybe," he said, offering her his arm. "Now why don't we go get those tacos?"

She wanted to cry, but then she would mess up the makeup that Chastity had so skillfully put on her. Wrapping her arm through his, she let him lead her outside.

She fully expected his truck to be waiting for her outside,

but instead there was a horse-drawn carriage, and pulling that carriage, was Hyacinth, pretty pink ribbons tied in her mane and tail. Sophia didn't even know what to say and could only playfully tug at his arm.

"I know, I know. But this part was for me. Can I help it if I want to treat you like a princess?"

It was cheesy, but how could she mind? Tears really did well up, and he kissed her cheek before leading her to the carriage and helping her in.

"So, what taco stand are we pulling up to in a horse-drawn carriage?"

"Oh, I never said we'd go to a taco *stand*."

She knew that tone. That tone meant he was up to something. "Bradley... what are you planning?"

"You'll see."

She wanted to ask more, but he looked so pleased with himself that she decided to let him have his fun. Sitting back, she enjoyed her carriage ride through the city.

How had her life changed so much in just a couple of years? She'd gone from homeless and on the run to a literal fairy tale. She wasn't going to ever forget that, and she wanted to pass that onto other people. Maybe open a shelter or run a program. Something that helped people like her.

But first things first, and that was whatever Bradley was planning. They pulled up to a fancy hotel, the kind that she could never afford before, and he helped her down. Arm in arm, they headed in and walked a fancy silver carpet that was laid out for them until they ended up at a set of giant doors.

"Is this it?" she asked.

"Yeah, this is it."

He nodded to Chastity and Missy behind him—who had

followed over in Missy's truck. And they rushed around to open the doors. Together, the couple walked into what Sophia could only describe as a reception right out of her notebook.

"Sophia!"

She knew that voice.

Her breath caught, and she looked towards the sound to see her mother, her real, actual mother, dressed in a gray mother-of-the-bride dress. Letting go of Bradley, she rushed towards her mom and threw her arms around her.

"Mom! I'm so excited to see you! Wait, you were able to get off work? I thought your boss wouldn't give you any more days off?"

"When your husband called me, telling me what he was planning, how could I say no?"

"Wait, you planned this?"

He smiled bashfully. "Well, I know it wasn't exactly like everything in your notebook. But it seemed to me like the most important part of the whole wedding thing was this part, the celebration. And I figured you'd be ready with that monster going to prison."

"But what if he wasn't found guilty?"

"He was going to be. I knew it."

Well, she couldn't argue with that.

"Come here," she said, letting go of her mother and crooking her finger at him. A moment later, his arms were wrapping around her and they were kissing again.

She felt so full that it was almost like her heart was going to burst. This was exactly what she had always wanted but never dared to admit to herself. The whole world was in front of her at the moment, and she couldn't be more content.

She guessed that it really was a fairy tale, after all.

Except her story wasn't ending. It was just beginning.

And she couldn't wait.

Especially since she was willing to bet that Bradley had arranged the honeymoon too.

~

HELLO READER! I hope you loved Bradley and Sophia's love story. Ready to read about the final Miller brother of Montana? Book Five, Taming Her Cowboy Billionaire, is ready for you to read. It's all about the youngest brother Bryant becoming humbled and finally deciding it's time to come back to his roots. Keiko is in this one too and there's a lot to her once Bryant gets to know her better. I think you're going to love this story!

You can find Bryant and Keiko's love story on all major retailers. Plus, you can find it on my own online bookstore if you'd like to support my small mom-owned business. I'd be honored if you chose to do so. Scan the QR code below to be taken to Taming Her Cowboy Billionaire at Natalie Dean Books. If scanning QR codes isn't your thing, you can also find my store here: nataliedeanbooks.com

ABOUT THE AUTHOR

Born and raised in a small coastal town in the south, I was raised to treasure family and love the Lord. I'm a dedicated homeschooling mom who loves to travel and spend time with my growing-up-too-fast son.

When I'm not busy writing or running my business, you can find me cleaning house, cooking dinner, feeding our three rescue cats, trying to make learning fun and coaxing my son to pick up his toys. On less busy days, you may also find me paddling down a spring run in Florida, hiking a mountain trail in Georgia (on the rare vacation to the mountains), or enjoying a book.

If you love Natalie Dean books, you can be notified of new releases by signing up to my newsletter at nataliedeanauthor.com, where you will also receive two free short stories for signing up. Just click on the "Free Books" tab at the top and you'll be on your way!

Also, as previously mentioned, I've opened my own online bookstore and I'd love your support! As of June 2024, I'm selling my ebooks at Natalie Dean Books. By late summer or fall 2024, I should have audiobooks, regular paperbacks, large print paperbacks, dyslexic print paperbacks and signed paperbacks all available. At the request of my loyal readers, I'll also be adding merchandise, such as glasses, cups, magnets and more. So come check out my small mom-owned author business at nataliedeanbooks.com.

You can also scan the QR code below to be taken to the home page of Natalie Dean Books.

f facebook.com/nataliedeanromance